WHERE DO YOU STOP?

Also by Eric Kraft

Herb 'n' Lorna

Reservations Recommended

Little Follies

WHERE DO YOU STOP?

The
PERSONAL HISTORY,
ADVENTURES, EXPERIENCES
&
OBSERVATIONS
of
PETER LEROY
(CONTINUED)

BY

ERIC KRAFT

Picador USA ✹ New York

Picador® is a U.S. registered trademark and is used by St. Martin's Press under license from Pan Books Limited.

Book design by Eric Kraft

ISBN 0-312-11932-1

First published in the United States by Crown Publishers, Inc.

First Picador USA Edition: March 1995
10 9 8 7 6 5 4 3 2 1

For Mad

Here am I, lying under a hayrick. The tiny narrow spot I'm taking up is so infinitesimally small by comparison with the rest of space, where I am not and which has nothing to do with me, and the portion of time which I may succeed in living through is so insignificant when confronted with eternity, wherein I was not and shall not be. Yet within this atom, this mathematical point, the blood is circulating, the brain is working, something or other yearns. . . .

Bazarov, in Ivan S. Turgenev's *Fathers and Sons*
(translated by Bernard Guilbert Guerney)

The interaction between thought and language always fascinated Bohr. He often spoke of the fact that any attempt to express a thought involves some change, some irrevocable interference with the essential idea, and this interference becomes all the stronger as one tries to express oneself more clearly. Here again there is a complementarity, as he frequently pointed out, between clarity and truth—between *Klarheit und Wahrheit*, as he liked to say. This is why Bohr was not a very clear lecturer. He was intensely interested in what he had to say, but he was too much aware of the intricate web of ideas, of all possible cross-connections; this awareness made his talks fascinating but hard to follow.

Victor F. Weisskopf, "Niels Bohr, the Quantum, and the World"
(from *Niels Bohr: A Centenary Volume*)

Electrons exist both on their own, as free particles, and as constituents of atoms, and they can change from one role to the other and back. An electron forming part of a carbon atom in the skin of your wrist could be knocked out of position by a passing cosmic ray and become part of the tiny electric current in your digital wristwatch, and then in turn become part of an oxygen atom in the air you breathe as you raise your arm to look at the time.

Frank Close, Michael Martin, and Christine Sutton, *The Particle Explosion*

In the [scanning tunneling microscope] the "aperture" is a tiny tungsten probe, its tip ground so fine that it may consist of only a single atom. . . . Piezoelectric controls maneuver the tip to within a nanometer or two of the surface of a conducting specimen—so close that the electron clouds of the atom at the probe tip and of the nearest atom of the specimen overlap.

H. Kumar Wickramasinghe, "Scanned-Probe Microscopes"
(*Scientific American,* October 1989)

Simmel, on the basis of a partial reading of Nietzsche, recognizes this in his Metaphysics of Death: "The secret of form lies in the fact that it is a boundary; it is the thing itself and at the same time the cessation of the thing, the circumscribed territory in which the Being and the No-longer-being of the thing are one and the same." If form is a boundary, there then arises the problem of the plurality of boundaries—and the calling them into question.

Manfredo Tafuri,
The Sphere and the Labyrinth:
Avant Gardes and Architecture from Piranesi to the 1970s

The right thing and the time it takes are connected by a mysterious force, just like a piece of sculpture and the space it fills.

Robert Musil, *The Man Without Qualities*
(translated by Eithne Wilkins and Ernst Kaiser)

WHERE DO YOU STOP?

Preface

SOMETIMES MY MEMORY seems to be mush, with shining moments scattered through it like chips of marble in wet cement or peas stirred into mashed potatoes. I'd like to be able to take a closer look at some of those moments, but whenever I reach for one I disturb the mush, and the moment I seek sometimes sinks out of sight. I reach, I scoop, I grab. Sometimes I get what I'm after, but more often I come up with nothing but mush, or I get hold of a different moment, not the one I wanted. Reaching for a chip of marble, I come up with a pea. Once in a while, though, something—some random turbulence in the mush, perhaps—brings to the top a chip that surprises me, one I haven't looked for, but one I'm happy to see, like the one that surfaced on a fall morning about two years ago while I was sitting in the sun, reading the Babbington *Reporter*—the chip that led me to write this book.

Albertine's parents were visiting, it was a fine morning, and we were all having breakfast on the new deck behind the hotel. Albertine and I have come to enjoy the early days of fall more than any other part of the year. The weather is still fine but there are few guests at the hotel, so there isn't all that much for us to do—beyond entertaining her parents on their annual visit.

Mr. and Mrs. Gaudet—Martin and Anna—are very fond of me, and I milk their fondness for all it's worth. That morning, I was lingering over my breakfast, enjoying the sun. Martin padded into the kitchen to fetch me more coffee, Anna spread marmalade on my high-fiber toast, and I turned to "We Pay a Call," the *Reporter*'s weekly interview with an interesting Babbingtonian. That week, the *Reporter* had called on Vivian Stillwell, only daughter of the entertainers Florence Hill and Fred Lucas. Flo and Freddie, as they'd been known professionally, had been enormously popular as radio performers and, later, in the early days of television, ended their career as co-hosts of a daytime show. The interviewer wanted to talk about Vivian's collection of Flo-and-Freddie memorabilia, but Vivian kept trying to steer him away from what she referred to as "that old junk" and into the cellar, where she had her laboratory, her cold fusion experiments, and her homemade scanning tunneling microscope, or STM. Vivian's STM allowed her to examine matter on an atomic scale, thanks to a tungsten probe cunningly sharpened to a point just a single atom across. When she applied voltage to this probe, electrons left the tip and, exploiting some quantum-mechanical hocus-pocus, "tunneled" across the narrow gap between the probe and the specimen. While Vivian guided the probe across the specimen in a raster pattern, a system of piezoelectric controls, a feedback generator, and some other clever gadgetry produced images so fine that they allowed her to see individual atoms. All that I found interesting enough, but here's the part that really got me. "To begin a scan," said Vivian with undisguised pride, "I've got to maneuver the tip of the probe into position only about one nanometer—that's a billionth of a meter, pal—above the specimen—so close that the electron clouds of the atom at the tip of the probe and of the nearest atom of the specimen overlap."

When I read those words, my jaw dropped, and I let the *Reporter* fall into my lap. My eyes drifted out of focus. A feeling of the most pleasant nostalgia spread through me. An extremely vivid pictorial memory lit up my mind's eye like the final starburst at the end of the annual Clam Fest fireworks display. A little smile formed on my face.

"Peter!" said Mrs. Gaudet.

"What?" I said, or squeaked, certain that the little smile had betrayed my thoughts, thoughts best kept from Albertine's mother.

"Your toast," she said. "It's getting cold."

"Oh," said I, relieved. "That. Well. That's nothing."

"Nothing?" she said.

"I mean—thank you. Thank you. I—was just—ah—"

"You've been in another world," she said. "I know."

"You mean the—uh—the way I kind of drifted off?" I said. "I can explain that—I—"

"Your head's in the clouds," said Anna. "I know what you were thinking about, too."

"Heh-heh-heh," said I. "Well, Anna, you're a woman of the world. I'm sure you understand that—"

"The next book," she said triumphantly.

"I guess you caught me," I said, relieved that she hadn't.

"Oh, I know how your mind works," she claimed. "I've known you quite a long time, Peter. I can tell what you're thinking by the expression on your face."

I said nothing at all to that, just smiled and ate my toast and drank my coffee, but the truth was that the little smile that had nearly given me away came from the dazzling memory of Miss Rheingold's legs.

Miss Rheingold's legs had come to mind because Vivian Stillwell's description of her atomic-level imaging system had made me say to myself, "Hey, wait a minute! If the electron clouds of an atom in the tip and the closest bit of the specimen overlap, what has happened to the boundary between tip and specimen? How can we say where the tip stops and the specimen starts?"

That thought immediately led to another. It made me think of an old obligation undischarged: the paper I was supposed to write for Miss Rheingold, who taught me general science for part of the seventh grade and had those unforgettable legs. From that beginning I rambled on and on and on through that time of my life. It wasn't long before I came upon something that made me laugh out loud.

"What's so funny?" said a voice, but the wrong voice for the memory.

"Huh? What?" I said, looking around. I had expected to hear the voice of my old friend Raskol, as a boy, calling to me from a rickety tower on a hilltop in the middle of a grove of bamboo, but it was Albertine's father who was asking me the question, smiling at me from across the bistro table where we sat. "Oh," I said. "I'm sorry, Martin. It's—um—well, Anna can tell you—it's just as she said—I'm thinking of the next book—in fact, I'm thinking of the end of the next book."

This time I was telling the truth. I closed my eyes and resumed

my backward ramble until I found myself standing in a locker in the
Purlieu Street School, in the heat of an August night. Because I was
ten, I fit in a locker, though without much space to spare. If I
moved, the coat hook would poke into the back of my neck, but I
didn't move much, because I didn't want to make any noise. I was
where I wasn't supposed to be, and I couldn't allow myself to be
discovered. I was not afraid, though. I was thrilled. I was playing a
game with the watchman. I was thrilled, too, as an adult reliving the
moment, because I knew what I couldn't have known at the time,
that while I was there, hiding in that locker, I was gathering impressions that would lead—a year later—to my inventing a game and
thereby to my building a permanent memorial, a beacon, marking a
single moment of my childhood. This memorial beacon would also
be my seventh-grade science project, the final requirement of my
general science paper, though at the time when I was standing in the
locker the paper hadn't been assigned yet, and when it was assigned
it would take about thirty-five years to finish.

THINGS LEFT UNDONE—how they haunt us. At any rate, they
haunt me. I've noticed that they don't haunt everyone else. A great
many people seem to be able to walk through their days without
hearing at their heels the dogged shuffle of neglected duties, but I
am not a member of that lighthearted crew. The things I ought to
have done are there behind me always, each with a hook in me,
holding on with a thin but sturdy line, dragging along behind me, a
nagging reminder of a debt I ought to pay to the past before I pack
up and move on to something new. So, it is a happy occasion when
I get an opportunity to clip one of those strings and leave a millstone
in the dust.

I had left Miss Rheingold's general science paper unfinished all
those years ago because its requirements were so daunting and bewildering. It was much more demanding than anything I had encountered in school before I encountered Miss Rheingold. For one
thing, the paper had to be quite long, and until she came along my
classmates and I had grown accustomed to working in a shorter
form—one side of a sheet of paper with widely spaced lines. I liked
that form just fine. I could take in all my work at a glance and check

it for the seamless integration of ideas that I worked to achieve. Now I was going to have to blather on about a single subject for far longer than I thought I could.

For another thing, the paper had no fixed deadline. We were to turn it in when we thought it was ready for Miss Rheingold to read. This meant that we had to impose a kind of discipline on ourselves that none of us was accustomed to: we had to work until the job was finished—but we didn't really know what finished meant. We had never had to decide when a job was finished before. It had been finished when the time was up. Finished meant no more than ended. Often it just meant that the bell had rung.

For yet another thing—and this is the main thing that kept me from turning the paper in while Miss Rheingold was still around to receive it—the paper had to include a project, either an experiment or a demonstration, that illustrated its thesis. I didn't devise a project that satisfied me until after the school year was over and Miss Rheingold was gone (in fact, I didn't even realize that the project I had devised was the project I needed to complete my paper until that morning when I was sitting on the deck with Albertine's parents, remembering Miss Rheingold's legs).

Finally, and most exasperatingly, the paper had to answer an enormous, nearly imponderable question, the one that is the title of this book. If it seems like a simple question to you, try thinking about it with a ten- or eleven-year-old brain. Well, where *are* the edges of things? Where in space-time, for instance, does one phase of your life end and another begin? Where do you mark the onset of an idea, a discovery? Where do you mark the end of a belief? Where does my table end and the keyboard of my computer begin? Vivian's description of her homemade STM set me to pondering such questions all over again, and that was the start of my work on this book—or was it? Perhaps my work on this book really started with my work on Miss Rheingold's science assignment. Perhaps it began even earlier. Regardless of when it began, it is now, I think, finished at last.

I am astonished at how long this book became. I tried to cut some of the details, but I couldn't eliminate split session, the broadcasting career of Flo and Freddie, the drumlin in our back yard, my lighthouse, the terrazzo floor of the Purlieu Street School, splines, green blackboards, Miss Rheingold's legs and perfume, the smell of new pencils, shandy, Quanto the Minimum, *Elementary Introductory Physics Made Easy for Beginners (Book One)*, Marvin's mother's redfish court bouillon, my mother's business ventures, fried baloney, Ariane's hip, or Kap'n Klam's flirtation with hamburgers, and despite my cuts I think there may still be too many gadgets in here, but I couldn't eliminate any of the ones that appeared on "Fantastic Contraptions," or the windup record player, the combination locks on the lockers in the school, the flour bomb, my Shackleton Superba, the Lodkochnikovs' television set, or the windflowers, and so this book is as long as it is, which is, I hope, just as long as it ought to be.

(By the way: it has been my habit, heretofore, to tell my tale in installments of nearly equal length, the length of novellas. This installment is the equivalent of three of those. If it actually *were* three of those, instead of the seamless construction it is, they would have had the titles "Quanto the Minimum," "Ariane's Hip," and "Night Watchman." You may want to look for the boundaries.)

Peter Leroy
Small's Island
February 8, 1991

1

I WAS STANDING IN A LOCKER in the Purlieu Street School on
an August night, when a locker was a hot place to be. I was ten. I
would be attending the Purlieu Street School in the fall, when I started seventh grade, if the building was finished in time.

The Purlieu Street School was supposed to get the schoolchildren
of Babbington—my home town, the clam capital of America—off
split session once and for all. Split session was a means of fitting
more students into a crowded school system than it ordinarily would
hold. Since the end of World War II, Babbington had been growing
so quickly that people couldn't adjust their thinking to it, growing
"by leaps and bounds," as people said then. In developments all
over town, carpenters built houses furiously. The air resounded
with their hammering. Families moved into the new houses as fast
as they went up. During the sixth grade, a new boy or girl seemed to
show up in class every week. The schools were chronically over-
crowded, and about once a year the need to build yet another one
took everyone by surprise.

The point when a new school was necessary always arrived before the point when it was built, and no one recognized the point of
necessity until it was past, although I think that if the computational
power had been available the point of necessity might have been
predicted, since each child was an atom, a mathematical point, in the
social scale of things. Each newborn, each child reaching school
age, each child reaching a certain grade level could have been plot-
ted on a graph as a point, and if that had been done, then there would
certainly have been a singular child on that graph whose arrival in
Babbington, by birth or immigration, could be predicted to break the

back of the system, one child for whom there would be no floor space at nap time in the Babbington kindergarten, no slice of meat loaf in the elementary school cafeteria, no locker in the high school gym unless another new school was built. Alas, in those days before integrated circuits on semiconductor chips, people had to rely on pencils, paper, mechanical adding machines, and brains, so the arrival of the child who broke the back of the system was always a surprise, and it always precipitated a scramble to build a new school.

In the period between the time when the need for a new school was finally recognized and the time when that new school actually opened, space was often so short that the sessions were split: half the students went to school only in the morning, the other half only in the afternoon. I spent most of the sixth grade on split session. An advantage was that I was free to watch "Fantastic Contraptions" on television every day at noon. This program was hosted by Fred Lucas and Florence Hill, who had once been fairly successful in the movies, and then, as Freddie and Flo, had been enormously popular on radio, where they had a weekly comedy program. The Freddie and Flo Show didn't make the transition to television, and for a while their career seemed to be over. I guess they were lucky to get a job as hosts of a giveaway program in the obscurity of midday. It may have been Siberia to them, but it was the perfect time for me, since the noon hour was the gap between school sessions. On the shaky base of "Fantastic Contraptions" Freddie and Flo built a new popularity as scatterbrained humorists. Later, as their popularity peaked, they began appearing in special shows on nighttime television, too, but they were different people there, and everything they did at night was cautious, calculated, and aimed at adults. The Flo and Freddie I admired were not the Flo and Freddie of their nighttime specials, not the Flo and Freddie of strained artiness and pronounced significance who are trotted out now and then in television biographies illustrated with clips from those specials. I preferred the everyday variety—improvisational, quick, uneven, occasionally silly, always fascinating.

The giveaway program, a feature of the early days of television, was a type of show in which members of the audience were rewarded simply for being there. They didn't have to answer questions or perform stunts to collect prizes; they just had to show up. That seems unlikely today, I suppose, but the medium was very young then, and broadcasters were still uncertain about how to find and build an audience for it. Some genius must have realized that people would want to watch other people being given things, and that the viewers would come back again and again to see more people get gifts, especially if the people seemed to have done nothing more to deserve these gifts than getting themselves to the television studio, because it seemed to validate the ultimate in groundless hopes: that fate might reward a person simply for being alive. This genius must also have understood that it wouldn't be a warm, selfless pleasure at witnessing others' good fortune that would keep the viewers tuning in. It would be envy.

At first, the hosts of giveaway shows didn't do much more than chat with people for a minute or two before handing over some dishware or a reclining chair, but soon there arose an informal and undeclared competition. The people who chatted with the host began trying to be more interesting than their fellows in the audience: to be funnier, more foolish, or more intelligent, or even to seem more miserable than the others. These distinctions were rewarded. A set of silverware might be added to the dishes, or an ottoman to the lounger. In time, of course, the format for displaying or demonstrating one's distinctions from one's fellows was codified, formalized, and specified for each show, and the competitive type of show was born. This eventually led to the quiz show, but there was an intermediate type of show in which people had to perform humiliating stunts for cash and prizes. I do not count these as quiz shows since the contestants weren't required to know anything. This type of show enjoys a revival from time to time. Part of its appeal is that it allows the viewer to cluck and guffaw at the ridiculous lengths to which his revolting fellow creatures will go, the depths to which they will stoop, the humiliation they will endure for a few dollars or a car or a set of pots.

"Fantastic Contraptions" at first lay on the dusky line between the fading giveaway program and the coming competitive program, but over the course of its history it moved with the times toward out-and-out competition. In the first part of the show, amateur inventors

would bring their creations onstage and explain and demonstrate
them. This part was a lot like show-and-tell. One after another, the
inventors presented their gadgets. Then, at the end of the show,
each inventor would return and stand before the audience to receive
its applause. The one who got the most applause won a prize of
some sort. I could watch most of the show before I went to school,
but I had to dash outside and catch the bus, so I couldn't see the
finish, when the winning inventor was rewarded. For many viewers—not for me, but for many others, I think—the parade of gadgets
and gadget makers would have been boring without Freddie and
Flo, who made it hilarious. They had a running gag of behaving as
if they had just blundered onto this show, unprepared, and every
now and then, when something particularly outrageous occurred,
they would turn and look at each other, asking, silently, "How did
we get into this?" I would laugh at that look every time. The fact
that they could make me laugh at the same thing again and again
seemed to me a remarkable achievement. They also asked funny
questions about the gadgets and maintained a seamless line of ban-
ter, apparently improvised, that frequently wandered far from the
matter at hand, leaving the inventor standing to one side, puzzled
and speechless, wondering whether he'd been forgotten, until, after
a circuitous, hilarious, and sometimes quite personal digression, Flo
and Freddie returned, always, unerringly and brilliantly, to the precise point in the discussion of the invention that had set them off on
their ramble, catching the inventor flat-footed and woolgathering, to
the delight of the audience.

The fantastic contraptions on Flo and Freddie's show were mechanical or electromechanical. In every case, a contraption's announced purpose was accomplished—if it was accomplished—with
a great deal of clattering and clanking and whizzing and whirring.
Wheels turned, gears spun, armatures moved, bells rang, lights
flashed. Many—it would probably be more accurate to say most—
of the machines seemed to be failures. That is, they failed to accomplish what their inventors claimed they would. Many others seemed
to have no purpose at all, and their inventors never even claimed any
for them. When asked what the thing they held so proudly was supposed to do, they would just say something like, "Well, now, Fred-

die and Flo, I'm not going to tell you what this here gadget of mine does. I'm going to let you figure that out for yourself. [Here Freddie and Flo would exchange that look that got me every time.] What say we just flip this little switch here on the side and see how she goes?" I could tell, from the moment an inventor began talking along those lines, that the machine was going to be one of those that accomplished nothing, one of the ones that hummed and spun and rattled and clanked itself into a heap of scrap while the audience roared and Flo and Freddie exchanged looks.

Every machine, whether it had a reasonable purpose or not, included a lot of redundant or apparently useless parts. Off to the side a pinwheel would whirl, for example, catching the light, catching the eye, but contributing nothing at all to the declared purpose of the machine. I used to wonder, when I watched that distracting pinwheel spin and flash, what had gone wrong in the mind of the inventor. What had made him include this useless bit that glittered so dazzlingly, drawing attention to itself and its uselessness? How had the inventor allowed himself to get so carried away? Why hadn't he heard a reasonable inner voice telling him that enough was enough? When his contraption was complete and he stood back to admire it, didn't he notice this vestige of a lapse in his thinking, this souvenir of a stroll down a mental dead end? Wasn't he embarrassed by it? Apparently not. Apparently he didn't even notice it, though it stood out like Cyrano's nose. I noticed it, everyone else watching the show must have noticed it, and Freddie and Flo exchanged quips about it, but the inventor seemed entirely unaware of it, grinning helplessly in his ignorance, unaware of the cause of all the hilarity. I was embarrassed for him and others like him, even ashamed for them, standing in front of us with their mistakes showing, but Flo and Freddie never seemed to take advantage of them. Not at all. The oddities may have sparked their humorous remarks, but those remarks were never made at the expense of the inventor. They never humiliated the poor guy. Instead, they would seize upon the superfluity in the machine—its worst, most embarrassing mistake—and from it they would wander off into a rambling anecdote about Flo's bumbling uncle. This seemed to me wonderfully generous. Right in front of them they had the source of many an easy laugh, but they barely used it, just took off from it, and in doing so actually distracted us from it. Freddie might arch his enormous eyebrows at the superfluous whatsit, and Flo might flick it with a long-nailed finger and shrug when it spun uselessly, but then they would take off, leading us elsewhere, diverting us, making the useless appendix seem a small and forgivable error. I admired them for this skill and for the generosity that seemed to underlie it.

2

IT WAS MY FERVENT HOPE that my maternal grandfather, whom I called Guppa, a crackerjack Studebaker salesman and also something of an inventor, would someday appear on Flo and Freddie's show. I think I must have gotten the idea the very first time I watched the show, but I can't be sure about that; it's hard to pin down the onset of an idea. I pestered poor Guppa about it endlessly. At that time he was laboring to cultivate a garden plot in our back yard, so he was at our house most evenings, hacking away at the grove of bamboo at the foot of the hill, which made him an easy target for my pestering.

The hill was actually a mound created by the builder of our house. Before construction began he had scraped the lot bare and flat, plowing all the scrub pine and scrub oak into a mound that ran along the rear property line like a drumlin deposited by a retreating glacier. Tree trunks and stumps projected from this heap, and in it were gaps and caves to explore, but it provided my family more than mere amusement. It also gave us something to do, a mission we could undertake as a family: for nearly a year our Saturday occupation was supposed to be the elimination of this mound of debris. We never got very far. In time, weeds furred it, and it came to look something like a true hill, enough like a hill at any rate for my parents to accept it as a part of their landscape. In fact, since it was the only aspect of their landscape that varied from the smooth plane that the developer had created with his bulldozer, it became the proudest feature, and they stopped calling it "that mound" and began calling it "the hill." Then my mother, under the influence of an ad in a magazine, decided to make big money growing bamboo and fash-

ioning fishing rods from it. The hill struck her as the perfect spot for
a grove of bamboo, and that's where she planted it. From her venture we learned that the market for bamboo fishing rods was considerably smaller than we had thought and that once a grove of bamboo
gets a foothold the stuff settles in for the long term, expanding at a
slow but steady rate, annually claiming a little more territory. Our
grove had spread down from the hill and started across the yard toward the house. We would hack away at it as fiercely as we could
all weekend, but during the week, inch by inch, yard by yard, it
would grow right back.

My mother and I thought it might be best to give up and let it
grow, but my father had developed a grudge against it. "The stuff is
going to take over," he'd say. "It's just like the goddamned Com-
munists. You can't let them get established. Some day you'll know
what I mean, Peter. Some day you'll see."

When Guppa decided that he wanted to cultivate a garden, the
garden he had in mind soon outgrew the space he had in his own
yard. He decided to use ours, which was much larger. Guppa never
did this sort of thing by halves. He might have begun with the idea
that he was going to have a backyard garden like anyone else's—
some radishes, cucumbers, onions, peppers, and tomatoes—but in
his fertile mind ideas grew like bamboo on a trash heap. By the time
he approached my father with the proposal that he plant his garden
in our back yard, he had something considerably grander than radishes in mind.

"Wheat," he said to my father.

"Wheat?" said my father.

"Wheat," said Guppa. "Your back yard will be known as the
breadbasket of Babbington."

"The breadbasket of Babbington," said my father.

"Like the wheat fields of Kansas, fabled in song, but on a smaller
scale, of course," said Guppa.

"Of course," said my father.

"However," Guppa hastened to assure him, "within the limitations of scale, it will be just as magnificent."

"Sure, go ahead," said my father, to everyone's surprise.

"What I had in mind was to give you a share of the crop," said Guppa.

"That's all right," said my father. "I don't care about that."

"But there should be plenty for all of us," said Guppa.

"Okay," said my father. "It doesn't matter to me one way or the other. But I do have one condition."

"What's that?" asked Guppa.

"Beat that bamboo back to the hill and don't let it come back down across the yard." He picked up his paper and hid himself behind it.

SO GUPPA BECAME a sharecropper. He staked out a stretch of land running along one side of our lot, from the back of the garage to the foot of the hill. Every day when the weather was suitable for gardening he came over after work, wearing one of the identical brown suits that he always wore at work, suits that my grandmother, Gumma, called Studebaker suits, carrying a canvas bag in which he had his gardening clothes, a pair of overalls that really made him look like a farmer. When he had changed into his gardening outfit, it was easy to imagine him after the crop came in, standing in the field, watching the weather with a practiced eye, chewing on a stalk of his wheat. Until dusk each evening he worked quite happily with hoe and rake and spade. Under the pretense of helping him, I tried to make my case for his taking one of his inventions to Flo and Freddie. I urged him to rush home during his lunch hour to watch the show. To please me, he did, and then I chattered at him about the virtues and errors of inventions that had appeared there.

I discovered to my surprise that my grandfather was a shy man. He had no reticence at all about plunging into a Studebaker pitch with a complete stranger, but when it came to showing publicly the products of his own imagination, he was timorous and retiring. I wouldn't give up, though. I dragged Guppa through the entire inventory of his existing inventions and weighed them as possible Flo and Freddie items.

"What about the thing that raises the stuff in the drawer when you open it?" I suggested.

"That's not a complete success, Peter," he said.

"Aw, come on, Guppa," I said.

"Sometimes everything falls on the floor," he pointed out.

"Or on your feet," I admitted. "I guess you're right. Well what about the mailbox?" Guppa had rigged up the mailbox so that a light on top flashed if there was mail in it.

"That's a good one," he said, "but it's not my invention. I got it from *Impractical Craftsman*."

"Oh," I said.

I must have looked glum, because he said, "Look, Peter, I hate to see you disappointed in this. I tell you what. I've got a few gadgets in mind for the garden. While I'm working them out I'll be thinking about the show. Maybe I'll come up with something right for it."

"You will, Guppa," I said. "I know you will. I'm sure of it."

"No guarantees, Peter," he said.

No guarantees were necessary. I had already decided that if Guppa just put his mind to it he could come up with something that could get him onto "Fantastic Contraptions"—and win.

3

THEREFORE, IT IS NOT SURPRISING that when I found myself bored, when I didn't know what to do with myself, when I was a little on edge and needed to find or devise a way to relax, or even when I was just looking for a way to pass the time, I sought inspiration in junk.

Most of the time, I found it there. The ready availability of intriguing materials is, I think, a spur to creation more often than the arrogance of artists allows us to admit. Fortunately for me, I lived in a family where there was plenty of intriguing stuff around. My father and Guppa not only held on to a great deal of what most people would have discarded but scavenged and accumulated bits and pieces of what other people actually *had* discarded. They regarded any useless thing with the attitude that its true, deep, hidden, or overlooked utility would be revealed—eventually. This attitude was summed up in the words they muttered when they tossed the thing into a corner of the cellar instead of tossing it into a trash can: "Never can tell—might come in handy someday."

For me, these things already had their uses, since they were fodder for my browsing. I know that my mother understood the value of browsing through junk, because whenever she noticed that I was bored, didn't seem to know what to do with myself, was fidgety and at loose ends, or seemed to find time hanging heavy on my hands, she would suggest that I pass the time by browsing through junk. Oh, sure, she might begin more conventionally by suggesting games or puzzles, but if I showed no interest in that sort of thing she would say, "Well, then, if you have nothing better to do, why don't you straighten up the cellar," and I knew that "straighten up" was her way of saying "poke around in."

I HAVE SAID IT BEFORE: so much depends on chance. At my
mother's suggestion, there I was, down in the cellar, poking around
in the junk, when I came upon something intriguing: the remains of
an old windup record player. I don't know where it came from, but
whatever the source, it had, fortunately, reached our cellar in a state
that made it completely useless as a record player but ideal as a diversion. Thank goodness, it had no amplifying horn, no pickup arm,
no needles. If it had, I would never have seen it as raw material; I
would have seen it as a record player, and I would have been blinded
by that perception of it. I might have tried to fix it, and I might have
filled the afternoon with the effort, but I would probably have failed
and emerged from the experience frustrated, diminished by failure,
possibly scarred for life. Instead, thanks to the providence that had
dictated the evisceration and amputation of certain record-playing
essentials, I saw only an engine, just something that would make
something else rotate. Happy accidents had presented me with the
ding an sich and a tacit invitation to make of it whatever I would. Its
life as a record player was over, but there was a vital spark in the old
gadget yet. All I had to do was discover its true, deep, hidden, or
overlooked utility.

THE THING AS I FOUND IT was, essentially, this: a motor driven
by a spring that the operator wound with a large crank (see Figure 1).
The motor was mounted vertically inside an oak box, with the shaft
emerging from the top of the box. Mounted on the end of the shaft,
outside the box, was a platter, covered with green felt. The record
was supposed to spin on this platter, of course. A small lever beside
the platter moved a brake into position to keep the platter from spinning while the spring was being wound, or to release it to allow it to
turn. Mounted farther down the shaft, inside the box, was an intriguing trio of metal balls. Attached to each ball were two strips of
thin, springy metal. The opposite end of each of these springs fitted
into a slot in the rim of a metal collar that fitted over the shaft, one
collar above and one below the arrangement of balls. These collars
kept the balls in orbit around the shaft, suspended by their leaf
springs. The lower collar was fixed in position, and the upper one
slid on the shaft; however, its movement was restricted by a screw
that projected downward from the top of the cabinet, its end against

the upper collar. By turning a knob, I could move this screw in its threaded fitting and vary the location of the movable top collar. When the screw was at its lowest setting, the top collar was pushed closer to the fixed bottom collar, and the springy bands were extended outward, pushing the balls into an orbit more distant from the shaft, where their greater angle of momentum slowed its spin and, therefore, the rotation of the platter. When the screw was at its highest setting, the springiness of the metal bands brought the balls inward to a closer orbit and allowed the shaft to spin more quickly, rotating the platter more quickly, just as spinning skaters spin faster with their arms at their sides than with their arms extended. The adjustable orbiting balls acted as a governor, a limiting device. Their original purpose had been to allow the operator to keep the platter spinning at the 78 rpm of old shellac records, so the range of adjustment was kept short, just a narrow band at the center of the machine's possible range of speeds. The original purpose didn't in-

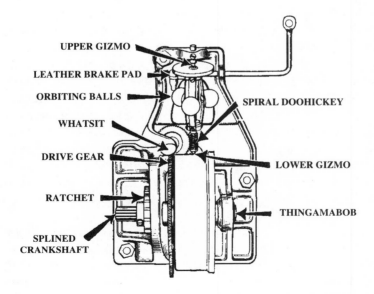

FIGURE 1: The drive mechanism of a windup record player like the one that I found in the cellar. Note orbiting balls that govern rotational speed. (Adapted from Part 3806, a diagram affixed to the bottom of a Victrola IV, manufactured by the Victor Talking Machine Company of Camden, New Jersey, January 1915.)

terest me, though. I wanted to see the machine spin at its extremes, so I began dismantling the governor.

By removing the adjusting screw entirely, I could make the platter spin much faster than it was ever intended to spin, and by doing away with the trio of balls I could make it spin faster still, quickly enough to catapult small objects from its rim. I tried this for a while, shooting things across the cellar and marking record distances on the floor, but I quickly reached the catapult's practical limits, and the record player vibrated so violently that it seemed likely to shake itself to death, so I gave that up.

More intriguing was the opposite extreme. With longer screws I could slow the machine down. When I'd inserted the longest screw that would fit, driving the top collar down against the bottom one, I thought for a moment that I'd slowed it as much as could be done, but a little thinking showed me the next step: longer arms, bigger balls. The balls didn't have to be mounted on the shaft, I learned; they could be mounted on the platter and they'd accomplish the same thing! It was the work of a happy hour to attach three dowels to the platter, each with a rubber ball at its far end. The system wasn't very well balanced, but it turned with majestic slowness, the balls bobbing gently as they orbited the center. The whole arrangement reminded me of the electrified model of the solar system kept in a glass case in the hallway of the oldest of the elementary schools in town. The school board had spent quite a lot of money to buy this model solar system and, fearing that use would wear it out, limited its public appearances to an annual demonstration before an assembly of students in the school auditorium, when we actually got to see the creaking mechanism turn. At the center, symbolizing the sun, was a naked light bulb. That, I saw, was what my gadget needed—a light.

I thought of trying a small table lamp, but my mother spotted me sneaking it out of the living room, so I had to settle for a flashlight. I taped the flashlight to the platter, wound the motor, and released the brake. Watching the spot of light moving around the walls of the darkened cellar, I realized that I had here the essentials of a lighthouse. I had wanted a lighthouse of my own for years. Now I was halfway there. I had the mechanism. All I needed was the shell, the housing, the lighthouse equivalent of the record player's cabinet. That couldn't be hard to come up with. Next to what I had already accomplished, it ought to be a snap. I didn't see any reason why, with some help, I couldn't build a lighthouse in the back yard in a couple of days. Of course, I would need my father's permission.

I HAD LEARNED that the best time to bring such things up was over dinner, preferably late in the meal. I knew, too, that I had to be careful not to give the whole plan away at once, since my father had noticed—and on occasion had pointed out to me—the fact that some of the projects I undertook didn't turn out quite as I had advertised them before I began. It would be best, I reasoned, not to announce my intention to build a lighthouse, especially since lighthouses were a touchy subject in my family. I'd once hoped that my father would build one for me, right through the center of our house. He'd started, but in the middle of the project he'd thought better of it—though I certainly wouldn't have put it that way—and abandoned the project. It would be best, then, to claim that I had something else in mind, something more modest. I asked permission to build a shack.
    "A shack?" said my father.
    From something in his voice, and from the way he stopped his fork on its way to his mouth and looked at me over it, I realized that I had chosen the wrong word.
    "Well," I said, "not a shack, a hut."
    "A hut?"
    Wrong again, apparently. "A fort," I tried.
    "A fort? What kind of fort?"
    Apparently, that wasn't going to work either. "More like a clubhouse," I said.
    "Oh!" he said. "A clubhouse. Sure. Why not?"
    At last. "Great," I said. "Thanks."

I SUSPECT that my father didn't have much faith in my ability to build a clubhouse or a fort or a hut, or even a shack for that matter, and that he expected me to build, no matter what I called it, an eyesore, because he allowed me to build it only if I built it at the top of the hill, where my failure would be hidden by the grove of bamboo.

4

I BEGAN THE PLANS for the lighthouse with that hopeful vigor we feel at the start of any project, when possibility is the driving force, the likelihood of success is at its highest, the project—in the mind—is perfect, pure, elegant, magnificent, clean, and right, and we seem to see, as if at the end of a tunnel, a shining day in the future when we will finish it and sign it.

In the course of a few evenings, I produced dozens of sets of plans. The first day's drawings were of a rather simple tower, something a crew of kids my age might manage to build. The second day's plans assumed the first day's and took the project to the edge of the limit of the capabilities of a crew of kids. Everything after that was impossible, but I couldn't stop. With each succeeding day, the tower grew and became more detailed. It wasn't just taller—it expanded in every direction. Each version had more rooms, more nooks, more crannies than the last, and before one drawing was even finished I'd thought of things I wanted to add to the next. The idea of the lighthouse was growing faster than I could diagram it, let alone realize it.

One afternoon I was in my room comparing the first and the most recent of my drawings and wondering how I had allowed myself to get so carried away, why no calm, quiet inner voice had told me that enough was enough, when I heard footsteps on the stairs. It was the rapid, unmistakable tread of my friend Rodney (Raskol) Lodkochnikov, of the river-dwelling Lodkochnikovs, baymen and boatmen for generations, brother to the two Ernies and the sultry Ariane. Quickly I hid all the drawings but the first.

"Hi, Peter," he said. "What are you up to?"

"Oh, just drawing some plans," I said.

"Plans?" he said. He took one look at my drawing and seized it at once. He was impressed.

"This is great!" he said. "This is really great."

I've never been good at accepting praise. I blush and stammer and look at my feet, just as I did then.

"A watchtower," he said. "Just like those prison movies. Great."

"Um—"

"With a searchlight turning on top and everything."

"You—ah—don't think it looks more like a lighthouse?" I asked.

"No!" he said. "Not at all! No, no, don't worry about that. A watchtower, definitely."

"It looks a little like a lighthouse to me," I said.

"Naaah!" he said, giving me a punch in the shoulder. "Not at all. Don't worry about it. It's terrific."

What was I to do? Raskol was my best friend. I looked at the drawings. A transformation seemed to have occurred. It did look like a watchtower.

"When do we get started?" asked Raskol.

I stalled. "I think the plans need some work before we can start building," I said. I needed time to make the thing look less like a watchtower and more like a lighthouse.

"Really?" said Raskol. "They seem fine to me. I can see the whole thing, plain as day."

That night we began scavenging building materials from the frontiers of the developments, where there was a substantial supply of scrap lumber, bent nails, and remnants of tarpaper. It wasn't long before we turned to the mother lode of scrap itself: the Purlieu Street School.

5

THAT'S HOW I came to be standing in a locker in the unfinished school building, in the heat of an August night, still and silent and happy and thrilled. The thrill of danger, the possibility of being caught, wasn't the only thrill. Prowling through the unfinished school building had made me begin to feel a thrilling anticipation of seventh grade that in memory is so thoroughly mixed with the thrill of danger that I can't quite tell them apart.

My hopes for a new school year had never been greater. I always felt an anticipatory thrill before a new school year, the anticipation of novelty. According to what I'd heard from older, bigger, wiser kids, the novelty of seventh grade was greater than that of any previous grade. I would find it newer than new, as the advertisements for soap, cars, television sets, and dog food used to promise in those days. There was one note of disappointment in all this pleasant anticipation, though. With the opening of the Purlieu Street School, there would be room for everyone again, and we would return to normal conditions. It would be the end of split session. I would be going to school for a full day, ending at three in the afternoon. I would miss Flo and Freddie.

The building in which I expected to experience all that thrilling novelty was located just a block from my house, in what had once been a pleasant field where ragweed and goldenrod grew so high that my friends and I used to wriggle through it for hours (or for what in an adult's memory of a child's pastime seems like hours), just wriggling randomly, in sinuous paths, invisible to one another, to see how often our paths crossed. Like all the other school buildings built during this period, the heyday of school-building, it was low and rambling, made of cinder blocks with a veneer of beige brick on the outside, and like the cars built in the same period, it was bigger than the previous model and had more gadgets. Among the Purlieu Street School's gadgets were a public-address system and amazing folding bleachers worthy of "Fantastic Contraptions." Raskol and I began by picking up bits of scrap outside the building, but one day we found an open window—or perhaps it was a window that we could open—and from then on we spent more time investigating the building than we did harvesting scrap.

A building that's a-building is a greater pleasure than a building that's a building: its mysteries are exposed, and yet they are still intriguing, still complicated, no less mysterious for their being exposed than a woman is less mysterious naked than dressed. With Raskol I spent many a late afternoon and Saturday in the school-in-progress, wandering through its mysteries, our adventures spiced by the presence of a watchman, something of a mystery himself, who roamed the cavernous shell apparently at random. His coming was announced by a laughable clamor—jangling keys, scraping feet, a hacking cough, a pause, a thorough blowing of his nose—so by the time he arrived we were invisible, hiding in lockers, in heating ducts, or behind stockpiles of mysterious stuff. At night this game was even better. The watchman carried a long flashlight that projected a powerful beam, in which great looming shadows of school furniture and builders' supplies arose suddenly from nothing, dashed along a wall, collapsed, and rose again, a beam that leaped across a corner, raced toward the place where I hid, hurtled past me, even, as now in memory, across the very door of this locker, through the louvers and onto my face, but the watchman missed seeing me, always missed seeing me, and lumbered on, ignorant of my existence. Hiding from the watchman was a delectable game, tingling with the possibility of our getting into some real trouble if he caught us, effervescent with the fact that he never did, that we always won. As Raskol and I understood this game, we were the only players. In our minds, we were everything: the center of the contest and all its area and edges as well. The watchman was just a dupe. When he had passed and we came out of hiding, we would wink at each other, deliver ourselves of theatrical sighs, and laugh silently at his ineptitude, but we never noticed what, with the finer perception memory sometimes supplies, I hear quite clearly now—the watchman's jolly chuckle, receding with his footsteps.

AS IT NEVER WOULD BE after classes started, the whole school was open to us when we prowled it in secret. From any point of view other than ours, I suppose, it was closed to us, but because all its parts were equally closed, once we had penetrated one barrier we had penetrated them all. We prowled everywhere, visited every classroom, explored the machinery rooms, knew every closet and storage room, poked around in every office. As the end of the summer approached, we began to resent the fact that we were going to lose our exclusive relationship with the building.

On one of our nighttime visits, we discovered that the entry hall had been laid with terrazzo, the flooring material most like life. To make a terrazzo floor, chips of marble are scattered in a soup of cement, like notable moments scattered through a life, and then, when the conglomerate hardens, the surface is polished so that the bright chips show to good advantage, glinting against the monotonous ground as notable moments do in the memory. We knew that on the first day of school a train of buses would discharge students into this terrazzo entry, so we wanted to lay claim to it, to walk all over it, cover it as thoroughly as we could, make certain that we would be the first kids ever to step on any part of it, mark it as our own before the mob got to it.

We walked, we marched, we hopped, we skated, and my mind began to wander in a direction that had become habitual—toward Raskol's sister, Ariane. She was on my mind more and more often. When I say that she was on my mind, I mean not only that I pictured her or heard her voice or cast her as the female lead in certain fantasies, though I did all of that, but there was something else, too, an accompaniment to these thoughts of her, something like the background music in a film, but an accompaniment for all the senses, a set of sensations that I cannot fully recall or describe, but which, it seems to me, resembled smoke, Scotch, silk, and saxophones. (This can't be true, since I hadn't tasted Scotch at the time, but it's as accurate as I can make it now, at the time of writing.) As a result, I had begun to feel awkward in Raskol's company. My awkwardness resulted not only from the fact that I was preoccupied with his sister, but from my unsettling discovery that the mere sight of him made me think of her, made the light seem to dim, summoned the aroma of smoke, the taste of Scotch, the brush of silk, a saxophone's moan.

I had drifted into one of my reveries of Ariane while we were gliding around on the terrazzo. This one involved my being in that very building, that very night, alone with her instead of Raskol. Ariane and I had been wandering around the building hand in hand and had come to an open window where the night breeze drifted in, bringing with it the pale moonlight. Standing there, dreamy-eyed, Ariane idly fingered the buttons of her blouse. One slipped open, then another, and—

"Damn!" said Raskol.

"What?" I said, or squeaked. Caught! Some look must have betrayed my desires. It wouldn't have surprised me if Raskol had said, "Damn it, Peter, button my sister's blouse back up—right now, this minute."

Instead he said, "Look at that," nodding back at where we'd been. I saw, in a slant of moonlight much like the one that had illuminated Ariane, footprints of terrazzo dust. Before, in the dark, we hadn't realized that a dusty residue from the polishing remained on the surface. Now we were tracking it through the school.

"Oh," I said, relieved. "That. Well. That's nothing."

"Nothing?" he said. "It's evidence. And we don't want anyone to know we've been here."

"Oh. Sure. That's right."

"Peter," he said. "Wake up. Snap out of it. You've been in another world. You know that?"

"Huh? Oh. You mean the way I kind of drifted off? I can explain that—"

"It started while we were skating around on the terrazzo. You seemed to skate off into—some other place."

"Yeah. Well. It's funny you should mention that—"

"I think I know what it is," he said. "What makes you drift off like that."

"You do?"

"Sure," he said. "It's that imagination of yours. Your head's in the clouds. Not just in the clouds—in outer space."

"Heh-heh-heh. I guess you caught me," said I, relieved to find that apparently he hadn't.

"You were probably thinking about—" Or had he?

"Look, I can explain, Raskol—" I said.

"The moon, right?" he guessed.

"Well, look," I said, still in the confessional mode, "I—"

"And Mars?"

"What?" I asked, beginning to wake up.

"And the stars," he said, "and—the whole universe."

"Gosh," I said, truly amazed. "I mean—that's right. Exactly right. How did you figure that out?"

"Easy," he said. "It was the moon that got you going. On the way over here. The full moon."

"Amazing," I said.

"Hey, I know how your mind works," he claimed. "One little thing gets you going, and you're off on a train of thought that makes lots of stops. Any little station that comes along—you're liable to get off and take the next train that comes through. No telling where you'll wind up. You've got a strange mind."

I thought it might be best to say nothing at all about this conclusion, though I was relieved that Raskol didn't know my mind as well as he thought, and I was flattered to have him think that I had a strange mind. It was a good time to change the subject.

"We can wipe up the footprints with our shirts," I said.

"Yeah, but that's only part of the problem," said Raskol. "We've left our footsteps in the dust on the terrazzo. We're going to have to put it back the way it was."

"What?"

"We're going to have to rearrange the dust," he said.

We returned to the entry, got down on our hands and knees, and, using our hands and puffs of breath, spread the dust around in a good imitation of its condition when we had arrived. Terrazzo dust is a demanding medium, fine and unforgiving, choking and dirty. I hope I never have to work in it again.

That left our footprints, extending down the hall. When we had finished wiping them up with our shirts, I was ready to call it a night and go home, but Raskol had noticed something new; "Hey," he said. "Look at those tags."

Looking down the corridor, I saw yellow tags attached to each locker, folded flaps of paper, like butterflies that had lighted there. I got up, pinched one, and opened it. On it was printed the combination of the lock that had been installed in the door.

"Hey," said Raskol from the other side of the hallway. "You see what's on these tags?"

"Yeah," I said. "The combinations."

He thought for a minute. "You got any paper with you?" he asked.

"Sure," I said. In those days I always carried a small wirebound notebook.

"Copy these combinations, okay?"

"All of them?"

"Yeah, all of them. Better get them all."

"That's going to take some time."

"Okay, we'll do them in shifts. You go on and get some, and when you get tired come back here and I'll take over. Be sure to write down the number of the locker, too."

"Okay," I said.

I wandered through the school for a while, jotting down locker combinations until I felt I'd done my share. When I got back to Raskol, he had one of the locks apart.

"And look at this," he said, as if I'd been standing beside him all along. "Just two bolts hold these locks in the door. See? You can take one off in a few seconds—if you've got the door open. Now watch this. This little cap with the numbers printed on it fits onto this shaft and over the splines."

Splines. What a nice word. This was my first encounter with it. It appealed to me at once. It seemed inherently poetic, sensual. In fact, it sounded so good that I could imagine lots of uses for it, none of which was related to combination locks. Splines could be soft, round, benign creatures, handy to writers as emblems of hope and calm: "When the storm abated at last, Cynthia and I emerged from the cave where we'd sought shelter. A preternatural calm had set-

tled over the sea, and the splines had come out to sun themselves on
the rocks." Just as easily, they could be the sort of rich, comforting
food that grandmothers specialized in: "Jimmy! Time to get up
now, you hear? Grandma has fixed you your favorite—hot splines
with butter and honey." My ignorance of the true nature of splines
must have shown, since Raskol went on to deliver an explanation.

"See these little slots inside the cap?" he said. "They slide onto
these ridges on the shaft. Those are the splines. They make the cap
turn the shaft instead of just turning *on* it."

Ah, splines. What a good idea. What a nice word. The idea of a
splined shaft appealed to me almost as much as the word. As a device, it demonstrated economy of design. As a concept, it suggested
security. *Spline* still sounds wonderful to me. That moment in the
empty school building when I first heard the word has stood out in
my memory ever since, and it gives me great pleasure now to brush
aside the dust of the intervening years and let this bright chip shine.

"I see," I said, and I wanted to add that I'd seen splines before, on
the shaft of the windup record player, but Raskol rushed on.

"Well, get this," he said. "There's a little mark here on the shaft
that shows where zero is supposed to line up. See?"

"Yep."

"But—when I put the cap back—if I turn it so that it goes onto the
shaft just one spline out of line—like this—see what happens?"

"Yeah," I said. "The five is where the zero is supposed to be."

He just stood there grinning.

"How long do you suppose it would take to change them all?" I
asked.

"Not long," he said. "But that's not what I want to do. Not now."

This surprised me. It seemed like a great stunt, the sort of thing
that would make us famous.

"Words of wisdom from my father," said Raskol. "Keep an ace
in the hole. A dollar in your pocket. Never let them know all you
know." I knew that he really did follow this last bit of advice. He
was wary about letting the teachers know how much he knew. He
always suspected their motives when they questioned him.

"This," he said, reassembling the lock, "is something to keep up
our sleeves."

6

WHEN SCHOOL OPENED, I entered the building through the front door with all the other students and immediately felt a great loss. The building was now available to just about anyone. Its hallways rang with the clatter and din of a vulgar horde—a vulgar horde composed largely of my friends, it's true, but they seemed like invaders nonetheless. The invaders wore looks of bewilderment, just like the look (I imagined with a mental sneer) that the foot soldiers of Alaric the Visigoth must have worn when they entered Rome. Merging with the rushing confusion, I caught sight of myself reflected in the glass of a door. I was surprised to find that I wore the same look. None of us knew it yet, but we were all going to be wearing that look for some time. There were four reasons—at least four reasons—why.

First, at some time during the summer we must have passed a boundary between childhood and adolescence, without even noticing it. I had had some vague realization of this as soon as I entered this new and larger school building. I felt that I was suddenly expected to be, in some way that I did not understand, newer and larger myself, more grown-up, more responsible. That was unsettling enough in itself, I'm sure, but time's longer view shows me now that it was compounded by the fact that when I looked for models of the grown-up and responsible behavior that the seventh grade was apparently going to require of me, I looked, more closely than ever before, at my parents, and I began to come to see—again, only vaguely—that they were imperfect models, quite possibly unequal to the puzzling demands of the seventh grade.

Second, I discovered to my surprise that the kids of Babbington came in a far broader range of shades of beige and brown than I had previously realized. I had known birches—and ashes and oaks—but now, in that instant when I came through the front door of the new building, the range was extended to include boys and girls of teak and mahogany and walnut. Here was a bunch of my contemporaries whom I'd never seen before. Where had these browner boys and girls been all this time? I think I realized—I think we all realized, at some level below words—what this surprising broadening meant: there was more to Babbington than we knew. Immediately, the unsettling question arose: how much more? How do we measure the size of our ignorance, after all? We don't know how much we don't know until what we don't know becomes what we didn't know; that is, after we know it; and then we know only how much we didn't know compared to what we know now—we still don't know how much we don't know. This was the first lesson of the seventh grade, taught the moment I came through the door. It might as well have been chiseled into the terrazzo that had been so thoroughly cleaned and polished for opening day.

Before that moment, I suppose I thought, if I thought about it at all, that I had Babbington pretty well figured out. Now here was new evidence of my ignorance. Sometimes my youth seems to have been devoted entirely to the accumulation of such evidence. Here was the revelation of a new world. I felt disoriented, much as I imagine a fifteenth-century peasant would have felt if he'd been handed a map at the center of which was something other than his little village, the center of his world. I remember well another feeling that came with this new knowledge. I was annoyed. I didn't like the idea that I had been kept in the dark or the notion that I was now expected to make sense of this larger world on my own. It seemed a lot to ask of a kid my age. I had begun kindergarten before I turned five and had skipped the third grade, so I was only ten-going-on-eleven. Perhaps, I asked myself, it would be possible to take another shot at the sixth grade and confront these puzzles next year, when I had matured? Not likely.

Third, there was imposed upon us a baffling new nomenclature. This frightening change made everything we were to study seem like an unfamiliar subject. Arithmetic had become "mathematics,"

and the word provoked an immediate mental image for me: a tightly wound spring, straining, powerful, dangerous. Reading had become "literature," and there was considerable disagreement about
how we were even supposed to pronounce it. Science had become
"general science," suggesting something vaster than science alone,
as if everything we had studied so far had been confined to a small
corner of a huge map now being fully unfolded for the first time.

The blackboards of the old school were absent from the Purlieu
Street School. In their place were devices much like them—extensive flat things mounted on the walls, meant for writing—but these
were green. What were we supposed to call them? Greenboards?
Green blackboards? Why had this change come about? The offi-
cial explanation was that yellow chalk on a green board would be
easier on our eyes. To Raskol, that seemed unlikely. "They're trying to confuse us," he said, and he sighed and shook his head slowly, as if his suspicions about the true purpose of school had finally
been confirmed by these green blackboards. (Years would pass before *chalkboard* became the general term, and during the intervening period of uncertainty the nation's youth, innocent victims of a
summertime revolution in the technology of wall-mounted writing
surfaces, sat puzzled through millions of student hours pretending
to listen to geography and geometry but unable to stop asking themselves, "What the heck should I call that thing on the wall?" In the
years since that time, I have found myself repeating Raskol's as-
sessment more and more frequently, in more and more settings.
When I arrive at an airport, for example, frantic and sweaty, certain
that I've missed my flight, and a smiling young woman in the uni-
form of the airline tells me that snow flurries at an airport half a
continent away mean that my flight won't be leaving for two hours,
Raskol appears before me, just as he was in the seventh grade. He
shakes his head, he sighs, he holds his hands out in helplessness.
"See?" he says. "They're trying to confuse you.")

Fourth, and possibly most bewildering of all, we were made to
change classes. When our day's bout with one subject had ended,
we got up and left the room, and went to another, similar, room
where we tussled with another, different, subject. What an enormous change this was. In the past, when we had spent nearly the

entire school day in one room, we had drifted from one subject to the next, one blending slightly with the next, like the indistinct edges of objects depicted in a watercolor painting, but the act of changing classes said, "There is definition here. Crisp lines separate one subject from another. The boundaries of knowledge are sharp and can be marked precisely," and here I am at the edge of my theme.

Mark Dorset, my sociologist friend, has said that one of the ways people can be divided into two camps is according to whether they exhibit a tendency to stay put or a tendency to move on. The difference between staying-put behavior and moving-on behavior is, he says, profoundly indicative of essential personality traits. Well. There we were, after six years of staying put for most of the school day, now required to move on every forty-eight minutes. A personality change was being imposed on us. We would be sitting in a classroom, stable and studious, and then a bell would ring, triggering a brief, intensely active period, a burst of frantic energy, when we all changed our positions, rushing into the halls like photons scattered from a naked light bulb, like particles of dust puffed into the air, or like a multicolored bunch of marbles in the confusing midgame in Chinese checkers.

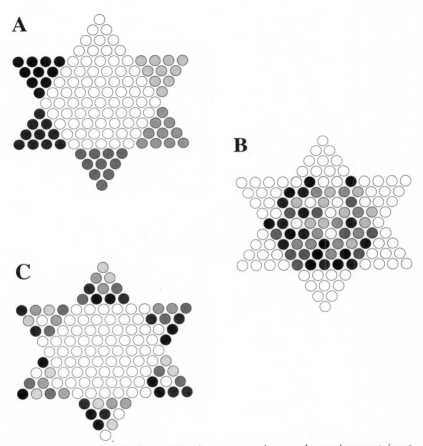

FIGURE 2: A game of Chinese Checkers among players who are ignorant, inept, or insane serves to illustrate several complex processes, including changing classes, mixing scents, and arriving at new ideas. (A) Taking the example of changing classes only: at time x six groups of students are seated in six classrooms, studying (clockwise from top) science, English, art, shop, mathematics, and history. (B) At the end of period x, a bell rings and the students surge into the hallway, heading for the classrooms where their classes for period x + 1 will be held. (C) In period x + 1, the students are again seated in the same six classrooms, studying (clockwise from top) science, English, art, shop, mathematics, and history, but they are, of course, not the same students who occupied those classrooms in period x. Now they are commingled, confounded, and confused.

7

BY THE TIME I reached general science, my last class that first day, I was in a state of high bafflement. I filed into the room with the others, found a seat, sat, took one look at the teacher, and sank into an enchanted gape. She was astonishing. She was blond, and she had, to use the terminology of the time, a gorgeous figure. I can't be certain just what the other kids were thinking, but she inspired in me a number of questions. What was she doing here? Why was this amazing woman, who ought to be in the movies or competing in a beauty contest, teaching science in Babbington? Was she lost?

Her name was written in looping script at the top of the green blackboard: Miss Rheingold. I felt an attraction toward her that seemed to be an actual force. I wanted to get out of my seat and go to her, get closer to her. I was aware, thank goodness, that if I did I'd be making a fool of myself, but still I had to fight the tug of her attraction. I'm sure I wasn't alone. All the others must have felt this tug. Yet it seemed to be specific, individual, meant for me alone. Trying now to explain something that was beyond explanation for me at the time, the best I can do is this: It seemed to me that whatever the other kids may have felt for her could only come from a spillover of her effect on me, that her force was directed at me, but that some of it missed me, sprayed out around the edges of me, and caught them incidentally, as I sometimes accidentally squirted my father when I was shooting my water pistol at another target.

Miss Rheingold was so full of enthusiasm that it showed in even the simplest thing, like calling the roll. She made this seem a thrilling event. I wanted to distinguish myself when I answered—I'm sure I wasn't alone in that desire—but "Here" was all I could think of to say, and it came out in a voice that shocked me by quavering. I wasn't afraid of her—nothing like that. I was thrilled. Did she wink at me when she glanced up from the class list to see who had answered to "Leroy, Peter"? I'm sure she did. It was my reward for being there and for being me. Never before had simply being seemed so fine. This was what it meant to be in the right place at the right time.

When she finished the roll, she asked, suddenly, without any introductory signal that we were shifting from the familiar to the treacherous, "Have you ever looked at the night sky?" She looked at her class list. "Patti?"

"Oh, sure. Yeah." This was comforting. We were all relieved. Looking at the night sky wasn't hard. It was something we'd already done. If general science was going to be on this level, we might make it through.

"How many stars do you see?" Miss Rheingold asked quickly. She took another look at the class list. "Caroline?"

Caroline said, "Oh, I'd say—"

Miss Rheingold rushed on. "How far away are they?" she asked, her eyes flashing. "Marvin?"

Marvin said, "Well, I guess—"

Caroline looked around the room in confusion. Why hadn't Miss Rheingold let her answer the last question? Something was going on here that she wasn't familiar with. None of us were. The problem, I now know, was that Miss Rheingold was so enamored of her subject that she couldn't see past it very well. She drew it to her like a lover, and the more closely she embraced it, the less she saw beyond it, and most important for us, the more oblivious she became to the requirement that she teach it. All she really wanted us to do was fall in love with it, as she had.

"How did they all get there?" asked Miss Rheingold.

"What?" said Marvin, still trying to decide how far away the stars might be.

"How far does the universe extend?" came from the Rheingold juggernaut.

"Thousands of miles," said Caroline, trying to answer Marvin's question, determined to get some kind of answer registered in her favor before Miss Rheingold hurtled on to the next puzzler.

"What do you think, Sylvester?" asked Miss Rheingold, glancing again at the class list.

"Biff," said Biff.

Behind me, Nicky Furman said, "*Sylvester?*"

"All right," said Miss Rheingold. "Biff."

Biff said, "Millions of miles?"

"What do you think, Matthew?" asked Miss Rheingold.

"To infinity," said Matthew. He seemed to be having a little trouble hiding a yawn.

"Do you know what infinity is?" asked Miss Rheingold.

"Sure," said Matthew. He was so eager to demonstrate how easy all of this was for him that he nearly sneered. "Infinity is—"

"Rose?" said Miss Rheingold.

Matthew's mouth remained open. His eyes widened.

"Spike," said Spike.

"Spike?" said Miss Rheingold.

"Spike," said Spike.

"Okay," said Miss Rheingold. "Spike?"

"What?" asked Spike.

"Do you know what infinity is?" asked Miss Rheingold.

"No," said Spike.

This made Miss Rheingold pause, but it didn't diminish her enthusiasm. "Well," she said.

She paused for just a moment, as if she were gathering her thoughts, but a glazed, ecstatic look came over her eyes, and when she began to speak, her voice had in it a breathless tremor that I recognized: she was thrilled.

"Infinity is really anything that is not finite," she said, "but I know that doesn't seem like much of an answer. In this case, you can think of infinity as a place so far away that it can never be reached. We can approach it, but we can never reach it. In the most general sense, infinity is any limit we can approach but can never reach. You know how a sequence of numbers increases."

We didn't, but years of schooling had taught us that we would have been fools to let her know. Instead we nodded our heads and made the confirmatory noises we'd learned to make to give the appearance of understanding—mmm, ahhh, uh-huh.

"Well," she said, apparently fooled, "a sequence like that approaches infinity if there is no limit on how large the numbers in it can become."

"Ahhh!"

"Of course, there are other kinds of infinity, too. There is an infinite number of points in a line."

"Mmmmm."

"And there's an infinite number of prime numbers, too."

"Sure."

"And, of course, the infinity of points in a line is identical to—but of a greater order than—the infinity of prime numbers."

"Uh-huh."

"Isn't that something?"

"Heh-heh."

"Infinity is also the place where parallel lines meet. What do you think of that? How can that be? How can infinity be at all? How can there be no end to something? How can parallel lines meet? Isn't this fascinating?"

"Mm-*hmmm*." We were exhausted. She was going too fast for us even to nod along in phony comprehension. Suddenly, her pace slackened, like that of a runner in a dream who suddenly sinks into a landscape of syrup.

"I used to love to think about infinity when I was a girl," she said, as if recalling an old boyfriend. "My friends and I used to lie on our backs and look at the stars and wonder how big the universe was and what was at the edge of it. The universe isn't infinite, though, Matthew. Of course, it's hard to say just how extensive it is, especially since space—well, space-time really, but we'll get into that later in the year—is probably curved, but anyway isn't it amazing to think that the universe has an end? If there is an end, then what is it? A wall? Okay, then, what's on the other side? Isn't this exciting? My friends and I used to love to ponder that one. Don't ideas like these send little shivers down your back, just thinking about them? Don't you feel a kind of nice wiggly feeling down in your—well, forget that. Anyway, these are some of the Big Questions, and Big Questions like these are what we're going to be exploring together this year."

Then, swept away by her passion for the Big Questions, she did two extraordinary things. She sat on her desk and she crossed her legs. Neither was done at that time. No male teacher would have sat on his desk or crossed his legs, but it was at least conceivable that he might. It was *unthinkable* behavior for a female teacher. To Miss Rheingold, the legs she crossed may have been merely legs, but in the moment of her crossing them they filled the room like the dazzling burst from a flashbulb. They were all that we could see, and their afterimage lingers in my mind's eye still. Say "legs" to me, and it's Miss Rheingold's legs I see.

Having caught our attention, she delivered a brief talk about the value and importance of science and the adventure in learning that we were about to undertake. I've forgotten nearly all the details of this talk—in fact, as I attempt to reconstruct it now, it seems to be largely about legs, which I know can't be correct—but I do remember that at one point she spoke about "opening our young minds." This sounded like a more direct and terrifying pedagogy than any that had been tried on me yet, and it made me a little queasy. A glance around the room told me that I wasn't alone.

"Now I'm going to conduct an experiment," she said, again without transition, "and I want all of you to pay very close attention." How it would have been possible for me to pay closer attention to her than I already was I could not—I cannot—imagine, but I sat up a little straighter and narrowed my eyes so that she would see how keen I was. "The reason I want you to pay close attention is that I'm not going to tell you what the experiment is. I want you to observe, and I want you to observe closely." More uneasiness. How sad it would be if our beautiful science teacher turned out to be insane.

She brought her handbag out from a desk drawer and placed it on the top. This too was an extraordinary thing to do, introducing a personal possession into the impersonal world of the classroom. I think that never before—and I scanned my memory very carefully before writing this—had I seen so personal a piece of equipment belonging to any of my other teachers. Then Miss Rheingold opened the pocketbook. In memory, I hear a soft male sigh from every corner of the room. If she would do this for us, open her pocketbook, within which, it was generally understood, the most intimate and intriguing feminine secrets were locked, what would she *not* do? What limit was there to her generosity toward us? How far would she go? From the pocketbook, she took a tiny perfume bottle. She set it on the desktop, and she removed its stopper, which she laid on the desk beside it.

"Now," she said, "let's talk about your science projects." I know what everyone in the room was thinking at that moment: What? What happened to the experiment? I know what everyone felt, too: She may be beautiful, but she's completely nuts.

"Please copy this into your notebooks," she said, and she began writing on the green blackboard. I still have the notebook in which I copied the assignment, in a handwriting quite different from my usual, an attempt to duplicate her loops and curves. It was this:

Science Paper

1) Answer the question as well as you can.
2) Include experiments that test and demonstrate the validity of your answer. (Thought experiments are acceptable.)
3) Include diagrams that illustrate your experiments and explain concepts.
4) Turn the paper in at any time, whenever it is finished. There is no deadline.

I glanced to the right and left of me to see how the others were reacting and saw many of them glancing around in a similar manner. I think it's accurate to say that none of this made any sense to any of us. We didn't know what "the question" was, for one thing. Nor did we have any idea what *validity* meant or what a thought experiment was.

"All right," she said. "Now you're going to pick your questions."

She was so delighted, so eager, that I felt relieved by this announcement. I should have been terrified. She brought out a spherical glass bowl of the kind that in those days was used to inflict a slow death on dime-store goldfish.

"The questions you will have to answer in your papers are in here," she said. "There are four copies of each question. That means that three other people will have the same question you have,

so when you pick a question you'll also be joining a group. Everyone in the group is going to work together to reach an answer to the
question that each person in the group picks."

I think it was right about here that we all began getting the first
of the headaches that would bother us off and on for weeks to come.

"All right," she said, "let's get started." It was clear that she
could hardly wait.

One at a time we came to the front of the room, reached into the
fishbowl, and drew a slip of paper.

When I bring to mind the moment when I reached into the bowl
to get my question, I experience it all again, not as memory, but as a
repetition of the immediate data of experience. I am there. I feel
the cool smooth rim of the bowl against the inside of my wrist, my
knuckles brush the inside surface, the slips of paper rustle, Miss
Rheingold shifts her position on the edge of the desk, and her
stockings whisper to me. I feel the thin edge of a slip of paper. The
scent of Miss Rheingold's perfume, diffusing from the tiny open
bottle, so much denser here at the front of the room than it was back
at my seat, makes my head reel.

I returned to my seat with the paper still folded, as instructed.
Miss Rheingold was having a lot of fun. The rest of us were tor-
mented by anxiety. When everyone had drawn a slip of paper, Miss
Rheingold said, "Now we have an interesting problem. We know
that there are six groups of four students who have the same questions on their slips of paper. How are you going to find them?
How will you figure out which of you are in which groups? How
will you discover who is in your own group? Does anyone have
any ideas?"

Matthew's hand went up at once.

"Matthew Barber," said Miss Rheingold.

"You could call the roll again," he said, "and have us read our
questions, and when you're done we'll know who's in our group."
He said this in such a dismissive manner that there arose around me
an incredulous murmuring and muttering. I had known Matthew
for years, and he had never really been a likable kid, but something
had happened to him, too, over the summer. He seemed now to be
merely visiting us, not to be one of us any longer, but to be a tourist

from another, better, place. He seemed disgusted by what he saw of the place he was visiting, and he seemed to find the natives here so stupid and boring that he could hardly bear their presence, hardly stay awake when they spoke, hardly stand to breathe their air. I wasn't alone in this feeling. There had always been animosity toward Matthew, but now it seemed to be tending toward real hostility. We were hurt; we were offended. We wouldn't have known how to describe his attitude toward us, but we recognized it for what it was: condescension, that putrid mix of contempt and pity.

"Very good, Matthew," said Miss Rheingold. "Very efficient."

Matthew beamed.

"Very efficient—" she repeated, and then she added, "—but not much fun."

A quiet cheer went up from the back of the room.

"What I propose," she said, "is this. I'll write the questions on the board. You copy them. Then you figure out how to find the members of your group."

These were the questions:

Where does the light go when the light goes out?
When is now?
What is the biggest question of all?
Why are you you?
What really happens?
Where do you stop?

We had just enough time to copy them before the bell rang, impelling us into the hall like so many mystified marbles, the image of Miss Rheingold's legs imprinted in our minds, the scent of Miss Rheingold's perfume wafting into the hall as we left, drifting, diluted, along the hallways as we walked away, mingling with all the other less exalted odors that fill a school hallway, some molecules of it lodging in the lattice weave of my shirt, to be shaken loose that night, when I undressed for bed, to bring her back to me, the dissipating scent of her arousing the indelible retinal memory of that moment when she had crossed her legs.

8

"WELL, PETER, how was it?" my father asked that evening, calling me from the bathroom where he had been soaking his hands free of gasoline and grease from the gas station where he worked. This procedure had fascinated me since I had first seen it as a child. It produced iridescent swirls on the surface of the water in the sink. My original thought had been that this was its purpose, and that mistaken notion still interfered with my attaining a conventional understanding of washing up. As far as I was concerned, it was still playing with water.

"It was—"

I hesitated. What should I say? Confusing? Baffling? Scary?

My father dried his hands and started on his way out to the patio, where he was going to grill some pork chops.

"Exciting, I'll bet," he asserted. "Starting a new school year is always exciting."

I was being invited to agree, I knew, but my father's statement surprised me, because he had never been much of a student, and he had never hidden that fact from me. Something had gotten into him, and I was too young to know that it was nostalgia. He dumped charcoal into the grill, squirted lighter fluid onto it, and lit it. While it burned he grew reflective. From his distant, unfocused look, he might have been thinking of Ariane.

"The smell of new pencils," he said eventually, as if something made him say it. "I always remember the smell of new pencils."

He seemed to be choking up. He cleared his throat and wiped his eyes. He blew his nose.

"Damned smoke," he said. He glanced at me to see if I accepted this explanation. I acted as if I did. "It's funny—whenever I smell new pencils, I feel full of energy. I feel that I'm getting a new start." He wore a wistful smile.

This was an awkward moment. I wasn't accustomed to seeing emotion in my father. I didn't know how to acknowledge it. I chose not to. It seemed best to say something, anything, so I started talking without thinking about what I was going to say. "In science—" I began, "I mean general science—we have—" I stopped. I had been going to say that we had a beautiful teacher, but I realized that it would be an inappropriate remark. My father, still wearing the wistful look induced by his memory of the odor of pencil shavings, was looking at me with unusual attention.

"Mm?" he said.

"—we have to answer the Big Questions," I said, putting the capitals in as Miss Rheingold had.

"The big questions?" said my father. He seemed not to have heard the capitals.

"Yeah," I said. "I'm in the where-do-you-stop group. Although actually I don't know who else is in my group yet."

"The what group?" my father asked.

"The group that has to answer the question 'Where do you stop?'" I said.

"What does that mean?" he asked. He seemed annoyed. The happy memory of pencil shavings seemed to have been blown away by this Big Question.

"That's the first thing we have to figure out. No—first we have to figure out who's in our group. But that's the second thing we have to figure out."

"What is?"

"What it means."

"Is this something special, Peter?" he asked. "Or is it part of your regular work?"

"It's—um—I guess it's something special," I said. "We have regular work, too."

"Well, just make sure that this when-do-you-stop business doesn't interfere too much with your regular work."

"Where."

"What?"

"It's where, not when."

"Don't get smart with me, Peter," he said. "Where or when is not the point. Is it?"

"Well," I said, "actually, I guess it is, or at least part of the point, because some of the other questions—"

"I mean that it is not the point of our little discussion here and now," he said. "The most important thing is that you do the work that's expected of you. You have a book to get through, don't you?"

"Yes," I said. *"Adventures in General Science."*

"And you're going to get regular assignments?"

"I guess."

"Well," he said, pointing at me with the barbecue fork, "you just make sure you do your regular work before you work on something extra. Now that you're out of grade school, teachers are going to start asking a lot more of you, Peter. Do you know what I mean?"

"The work will get harder?" I guessed.

"Yes," he said. "But that's not all. You see, they have your records. They know you're pretty smart. They know you did well in grade school. They're liable to use you to make them look good. You know what I mean now?"

I couldn't imagine how Miss Rheingold could be made to look any better than she already did, but if there was a way that she could use me in such a noble undertaking, yea, though it use me up completely, leaving me a dry and lifeless husk, spent in the task, I was ready to answer the call.

"Not really," I said, truthfully.

"If they give you some special project to do," he said, "and you do a good job, they'll look good. Get it?"

"Well," I said, "I guess so."

Would Miss Rheingold do such a thing? Was that what she wanted from me? Was that why she had crossed her legs?

THAT NIGHT, I got on the phone right after dinner. It took hours, but by the end of the evening I had identified at least some of the members of every group. A competition had developed when kids decided that anyone who succeeded in figuring out all the members of the groups would get on the good side of Miss Rheingold. As a result, there was a reluctance to give out information, and I was convinced that some of the information I had received was what is called today disinformation or misinformation, the kind of information that back then we called lies. However, by charting everything I was told and comparing it against what others told me, I was able to draw some reliable conclusions. By the time my father leaned over me, depressed the switch in the cradle of the phone, and said, "Peter, go to bed," I was sure that I knew who three of the members of the where-do-you-stop group were, counting myself. The fourth was still in doubt, but I had a pretty good idea that it had to be one of the mysterious black kids who seemed to have come from elsewhere or nowhere. I couldn't be sure, though, because I'd determined this only indirectly, by inference. I'd gotten my information from phone calls to my friends, and all the kids I knew were white. I didn't know the phone numbers of any of the black kids. I wasn't even really aware of their names. So, I didn't know how to ask them which group they were in.

IN DARKNESS, I groped my way upstairs to my room. It was a new thing of mine to leave the lights off when I got ready for bed. I've forgotten now just why I did this. Was it modesty? Did I think that someone was watching from the darkness? Did it have something to do with training the mind or the senses to get by on less information—was I already, unwittingly, anticipating the skills I would need for my game, that game that would lead to my commemoration of a single moment in the following summer, the same skills that I would need when Raskol and I finally got around to slipping into the Purlieu Street School some night and changing the combinations of the locks on the lockers? Or was it that I had begun spending a little while each night scanning the windows of the house across the street, where a girl I'd known for years as an annoyance was ripening into an attraction? It was probably that.

When I undressed, the scent of Miss Rheingold's perfume surprised me. In the dark, quiet room my shirt seemed to be saturated with it. When I took the shirt off and gave it a shake the scent filled the room so richly that I thought my parents would surely smell it. I held the shirt to my face for a moment and breathed the aroma, but when I realized that I was trying to smell Miss Rheingold herself, not merely her perfume, I began to feel weird, and I put it aside. I got into bed and lay there, awake, quite intoxicated, my senses full of her. I tried to recreate everything, every impression from the forty-eight minutes I'd spent with her. This wasn't at all hard to do, since my impressions were so strong. The memory was so vivid that its recreation seemed real, especially since it was reinforced by the sound of my father, downstairs, whistling and sharpening pencils.

9

I BEGAN MY RESEARCH the very next weekend. I've always been conscientious about such things. Give me an assignment and I get right down to it. I was one of those children who ate the lima beans first and saved the mashed potatoes for last, as a reward. I postponed work on the lighthouse until I had at least made a good start toward answering the question. Raskol was disappointed, but I wasn't. I was so eager to please Miss Rheingold that the lighthouse didn't interest me. He went on collecting materials and piling them in our garage.

"We'll keep this stuff in reserve," he said. "You never can tell when you'll change your mind."

"Sure," I said. "I'll probably get sick of this general science paper pretty soon," but I got down to work on my question with the conviction that I would never stop working on it until the paper was finished.

I confess that I expected to find that, beneath its daunting surface, the question would turn out to be no more than the sort of question I had always been asked in school, a question whose precise answer could be located in, and copied directly from, the textbook. I owed most of my early success in school to a knack for inverting questions, turning them into the beginnings of declarative sentences, and finding in the murky paragraphs of my texts the matching conclusions for these beginnings. It wasn't much more than a game, and not even a very challenging one.

So, I turned expectantly to my bulky new general science book. A slip of paper inside it instructed me in the proper way to open a new book so that the binding wouldn't crack. I had found a similar

slip of paper, with similar instructions, in each of the books I had
opened already. Even so, I read this slip carefully, and I followed
its instructions to the letter. There was always the chance that
they—and *they* figured prominently and frighteningly in the life of
a boy of the age I was then—might have slipped in a step specific
and essential to the proper opening of general science textbooks
and no other sort of book, just to see whether I was reading and
following the directions. They were sure to catch someone; it
wasn't going to be me. I wasn't going to have to confess to Miss
Rheingold on Monday that my general science book had come
apart in my hands.

"Miss Rheingold?"

"Yes, Peter? Oh, my goodness! Your copy of *Adventures in
General Science,* it's—"

"It sort of fell apart."

"How on earth—"

"I don't know what happened, I—"

"Didn't you follow the directions, Peter?" she would ask.

"Well, Miss Rheingold," I would have no choice but to admit, "I
did follow the directions, but I'm afraid that the directions I followed were the wrong directions. You see, I followed the directions for opening the English book."

I could almost hear her, fighting back a tear, say, "Peter, Peter,
this is a shame, such a shame. I'm sorry about this, truly sorry that
this has happened."

"Me, too."

"You know what this means, don't you?"

"What?"

"You're going to have to go back to the sixth grade. You've
failed general science."

In those days I was convinced that I was surrounded by opportunities for doing the wrong thing, and I knew from experience that I
usually didn't even notice I'd seized one of these opportunities until
it was too late. The difference between the right thing and any of a
million wrong things often seemed so tiny as to be nearly invisible.
Anything might trip you up, and it was more likely to be a pebble
than a boulder. I haven't had much reason to alter this conviction in
all the years since then.

The general science book was thick and heavy, packed with small print in two columns. I expected that the knowledge in so forbidding a book must be thick and dense itself—arcane, mystifying, thrilling, troublesome stuff, the very kind of thing Miss Rheingold's questions demanded—but actually the textbook wasn't any help at all. For all its bulk and density, what it held seemed to be much the same as what I had learned in just-plain-science year after year: quite a lot about tadpoles and frogs, but nothing at all about the edges of the universe, or me.

I went to the school library. It wasn't open on the weekend, of course; I slipped in through a window that wasn't properly secured. After all, since I had devoted a good part of my summer to discovering unauthorized means of entry, it seemed a shame that the opening of school should render so much knowledge worthless, and I welcomed this opportunity to restore its former value. Besides, sneaking in gave my research the thrill of the forbidden, providing almost as good a kick as I would have gotten if the subject of the research itself had been forbidden, providing something like the researcher's thrill I got when I poked through my parents' dressers or the stack of letters and bills they kept in a kitchen drawer.

The questions racing through my mind then seem still to be dashing about in there, bumping into one another like baffled students changing classes on the first day of seventh grade, just as chaotically mixed, the separations and boundaries between ideas just as hard to describe as the location of last period's science class after it has dispersed in the corridor: Where do I stop? Where did those dark kids come from? Why hadn't I ever seen them before? Where do I stop? Where are they now, those dark kids? Is that Miss Rheingold's perfume I smell? How did it get all the way up here to the second floor and into the library? Where do I stop? Is there some part of Babbington that isn't on my map, the part where the dark kids live? Where do I stop? What's my first class Monday morning? Do I have gym on Monday? Where do I stop? When are Raskol and I going to change the combinations of the locks?

My immediate problem, as I now see it, was that I had acquired over the years a number of overly simple ideas, ideas based on a view of the surface of things only, and they had become too firmly rooted in my mind—the solar-system model of the atom, for example, and the sectioned-map view of social boundaries, that sort of thing. Miss Rheingold's asking where I stopped marked the point in my education when I was first asked to think for myself. My mind was fertile, friable soil. New ideas were quick to root, and I was still at an age when old ones were fairly easy to uproot. Miss Rheingold's question had begun to tug at the simple old ideas. It hadn't yanked them out yet, but it had loosened them a bit.

I had a hard time keeping my attention focused on the question, though. I was alone in the library, of course. Need I tell you how distracting it is to be alone in a library? Unwatched, you must struggle continually against satisfying your curiosity about newts, heraldry, the merengue, combination locks—everything but the topic that brought you there.

Most of the books were not yet shelved. They were stacked and heaped here and there, on tables, window sills, chairs, and even on the floor, piles and pillars of new books. The appeal of books in a jumble, encountered at random, not shelved by topic and author, is enormous, far stronger than the appeal of books in ranks and categories. When picture books and gazetteers lie in a hodgepodge with poems, novels, handbooks of upholstery instruction, and photographic collections of examples of taxidermy, they make a rich, intriguing mix, something like gumbo or bouillabaisse, a stimulating concoction, a much richer and more intriguing mix than the array in the categorized sections of the library, where distinctions are made that wouldn't allow so many diverse and tasty things in the same pot. Those distinctions inhibit the browser, I think, and eliminate some of the potential pleasure of browsing. The gain from categorizing is order, but the loss is surprise.

Whenever I enter a library now I head first for the rack of new books, where some of the pleasure of the jumble still exists, before the books are made to quit the happy mix and dwell with their own kind. Having come in search of the latest biography of Wittgenstein, I'm as likely to leave with a treatise on the tube worms that dwell near thermal vents at the deepest points on the ocean floor.

That, however, is now. At the time I'm recalling, all that jumble and all those questions were more than my ten-year-old's mind could handle. There were just too many questions to answer, and the questions were radically different from the questions I was used to. Miss Rheingold wanted me to find an answer that wasn't obvious, that might not even exist. In the past, I had only been asked to find answers that were already highlighted for me. The feeling that there were too many questions and that I had to find answers where there might not even *be* any was new and unsettling, but it was only a foretaste of a feeling that would return, again and again, as a feature of adult life.

10

I SPENT MANY HOURS in the library before I admitted to myself that I wasn't likely to find the answer to Miss Rheingold's question in the books that were considered useful for students in the seventh grade. I had browsed pretty thoroughly, and I'd learned some interesting things along the way, but I didn't feel any closer to the answer than I had been when I'd first slipped in through the boiler room window. When I realized that a day had passed without my making any progress, I began to worry. When I began worrying, I found it harder and harder to think about anything but the stretch of time between me, there, at that moment, in the library, evading my work with a book about drumlins and eskers, and the day when I would have to deliver my report to Miss Rheingold. That stretch of time seemed elastic. I envisioned it as a rubber road, twisting and flexing sickeningly, extending into vague, dark space.

I wasn't getting anywhere and I knew it. I needed a break, and I needed some advice. Whenever I needed the refreshing boost that comes from another point of view, an unexpected idea, I turned to Porky White, as I still do. Yes, I mean *the* Porky White, the man behind the Kap'n Klam Family Restaurants that dot—some say blot—America from sea to sea, bringing the esculent mollusk within reach of one and all. I had known Porky for years. We met when I was in the third grade. He drove a school bus. I rode on it.

Porky had just opened his first modest restaurant—no more than a snack bar, really. He called that first place Captain White's. He hadn't become Kap'n Klam yet. I was an investor in the enterprise—on a small scale, naturally, a scale determined by my earnings as weed-puller, window-washer, and lawn-mower—but even so my status as an investor put me in an unusual relationship with Porky. He was an adult, and I was a kid, but I was one of his backers. It made me more confident in his company than in the company of any other adult, or even of other children I looked up to, such as Raskol. I think this showed in the way I talked with him. I was very forthcoming.

Not only was I a backer, but I was even responsible, I say with pride and what I think you'll have to admit is a disarming lack of false modesty, for creating—well, let's say *supplying*—the Kap'n Klam image. Porky knew that the business had to have character if it was going to succeed on the large scale of his dreams. In fact, he often said just that.

"Peter," he would say, "the thing is this—the place has got to have character."

"Right," I would say, since I'd heard this before and knew that he was convinced.

"You know what I mean?"

"Yup."

"Character is more important than class."

"Right."

"In fact, class doesn't really matter in an operation like this."

"Not really."

"It's not what our customers are looking for."

"Nope. Definitely not."

"I mean, let's face it, if they're looking for a classy evening out on the town, they're not going to be coming to a clam shack in the first place."

"No arguing that."

"I'm right, right?"

"You're right."

"But they want a place that's got character."

"Sure they do."

"If a place has got character, Peter, then they know they *are* someplace. At least they know they're not eating at home—you know what I mean?"

"Sure I do. Character. That's it. That's how they know they're not eating at home."

Porky had begun working on the character question well before he even had a restaurant, and I was an eager assistant in the effort. He got it into his head that the way to give the place character was to come up with *a* character who supposedly owned it. I suggested my great-great-grandfather, Black Jacques Leroy, whom I knew only from the stories I had learned from my great-grandmother, but who sure seemed like a character to me. I told great-grandmother's stories to Porky, and he and I decided that we might as well appropriate Black Jacques more or less as my great-grandmother described him, rather than going to the trouble of building an image from scratch. At first Porky called this character—a seafaring version of Black Jacques—Captain White. I think he got the idea, somewhere along the line, that this guy was *his* great-great-grandfather, but I didn't really mind. On the sign over the door of Captain White's and on the menus, napkins, and matchbook covers was a drawing of Black Jacques casually leaning against a piling, holding a beer stein. Porky and I developed a history of the fictitious Captain White, and he was the precursor, forebear, or first draft of Kap'n Klam, an old salt now familiar to virtually everyone, since he's pictured on all the paraphernalia of the Kap'n Klam chain. The enormous plastic statues of him that stand on the front lawn of every restaurant at home and abroad make my great-great-grandfather as familiar an emblem of American culture as Liberty.

That first Captain White's Clam Bar was a squat building on the edge of a clamshell parking lot behind a marine gas station, in the slovenly part of the waterside area of Babbington, near the mouth of the Bolotomy. The area had an authentic, atmospheric odor of rotting fish parts, a little touch of Babbington that is artificially duplicated in all 914 Kap'n Klam franchise restaurants to this day.

PORKY WAS SITTING in one of the wooden booths, flipping through some papers that I took to be bills of lading. I took them to be bills of lading not because I had any firsthand experience with bills of lading, but because I had encountered the term in my ramble through the unshelved books in the library, liked the sound of it, and welcomed an opportunity to use it, almost as much as I did *splines,* the need for which almost never came up, though the word had begun to make me giggle inwardly whenever I thought of it, since it inevitably brought with it, bound to it as if by a force as mysterious and strong as the forces that bind the diminutive components of all the stuff we are or know, the anticipation of the day when Raskol and I would change the combinations of the locks and baffle our chums.

"Bills of lading, huh?" I said, taking a seat opposite Porky.

"What?" he said. "What do you mean?"

"I—um—I thought those might be bills of lading."

"These? These are just the sheets that come with all the stuff I get shipped to me here—ketchup, tartar sauce, potatoes, that kind of thing. They always give you these sheets that list everything they deliver to you. I figure if they go to that trouble I ought to read through them, you know?"

"Sure," I said, happy that Porky seemed not to have noticed my ignorance. "That makes sense."

"What—did you find that in a dictionary or something—*bills of lading*?"

"A book," I said. "Not a dictionary, just a book."

"Peter," said Porky, "you want to be careful about using a term that you don't really know well enough. You can make a fool of yourself."

"Yeah, I guess so," I said.

"Some terms are much more dangerous than others," he said. "You fling them around when you really don't know what you're doing and people can spot you as a faker right away."

"I know what you mean," I said. "Like *epistemology.*"

"Well, yes," said Porky. "I guess so."

"And *ontology.*"

"Sure," said Porky.

"A lot of people get those confused," I said.

I had no idea whether this was true or not, but I loved throwing those two words around.

"And *fuck,*" Porky said. "That's another one you have to watch out for. But anything, even something as apparently straightforward

as *bills of lading,* can demonstrate that you're a guy who doesn't
know what he's talking about—if you *are* a guy who doesn't know
what he's talking about."

"How's business?" I asked, eager to get off the subject of my ignorance. "Are we making the big money yet?"

"Well—"

I took my notepad out of my back pocket. "Let me get the figures down," I said. "How many dozen fried clams last week?"

"I'm not sure," said Porky. "I—"

"Stuffed?"

"I haven't got those figures—"

"Gallons of chowder?"

"Say, Peter," he said with sudden interest, "how's school? New
school year! Unfamiliar surroundings! Strange faces! Surprising
things! Tell me all about it."

"Well," I said, "let's see." Mentally I scanned my new experiences, looking for one that would appeal to Porky. It didn't take
long for me to spot exactly the one. "There's a new science teacher," I said. "In fact, most of my teachers are new. Everything's
new, come to think of it. The water fountains are new, and really
nice too. They don't work yet, but I bet they'll work great once
they work at all. And there are two gyms. Two complete gyms.
Isn't that something?"

"Sure is," said Porky. "What do they serve you for lunch?"

"Oh, the usual stuff," I said. "But the science teacher, let me tell
you about the science teacher."

I knew that I had, in Miss Rheingold, a topic that Porky was sure
to be interested in. However, as soon as I began to frame my first
remark about her, I realized that she was a topic beyond my descriptive powers. No, that's not exactly right. I didn't *know* whether she
was beyond my descriptive powers or not. She was completely outside my descriptive experience. I had never had occasion to describe any woman before, and Miss Rheingold was a woman who
deserved a fine and precise description from someone with practice.
I had never even used the vocabulary that would be required. Those
were more reticent times, when it was not unusual for a boy of elev-
en never to have said the word *breasts,* for example.

"She has blond hair," I said.

This wasn't the powerful beginning I had hoped for, but it was a start. It had the virtue of staying on familiar ground, and it caught Porky's attention; he was at least interested in hearing what came next. It didn't do her hair justice, though, so I made another attempt.

"It's really light blond," I said, "kind of the color of—" I looked around the room for something that might help me out. "Lemonade," I said. "She has lemonade hair."

"Lemonade hair," said Porky.

"That isn't quite right," I said. "It's more like—beer."

"Beer."

"Kind of in-between. If I mixed some beer and some lemonade, I think I could get it just right."

"Shandy," said Porky.

"Hm?"

"That's what it's called. Beer and lemonade. Shandy."

Another good one: *shandy. Shandy, ontology, epistemology, bills of lading, splines.*

"I can picture it," Porky said. "Shandy hair. Very nice. What color eyes?"

"Um, I don't know. I didn't notice."

I brought her face to mind and stared at it, trying to see what color her eyes were. I couldn't be sure.

"She has a very smooth forehead," I said.

That had impressed me. It made her seem relaxed, even when she was dishing out science at her most frantic pace.

"It's *very* smooth," I said. "Round. Like a honeydew melon."

I was surprised to find how apt that was. Her forehead had seemed very like the skin of a honeydew—smooth, cool, pale.

"She has honeydew skin," I said.

I was beginning to feel a growing confidence in my descriptive talents.

"Honeydew skin," said Porky. "I like that. But that shandy hair—that was great. Delicious."

"And then her teeth," I said, getting up a good head of steam. "Her teeth are like—um—sugar cubes."

I seemed to be getting pretty good at this.

"The Captain's Shandy!" said Porky. He slapped his hand on the table. "The Captain's Shandy!"

"And her legs," I said, daring, thrilled, embarrassed, "are—"

"It's going on the menu tomorrow!" said Porky. "Peter, I'll never regret the day I let you talk me into letting you invest in the business. You're a fountain of ideas."

I couldn't think of a single suitable comparison for Miss Rheingold's legs, and I have never succeeded since, though my mind returns to the attempt every time I take a swallow of beer or lemonade on a summer's day or notice shandy on the menu board at a Kap'n Klam Family Restaurant.

11

I ARRIVED IN GENERAL SCIENCE the following Monday expecting the next step in the development of our questions and group work. I'm sure we all expected that. We expected continuity. Continuity was what we had been taught to expect, and we had learned the lesson, we *had* come to expect continuity, and we planned our little lives accordingly—do the next thing, that was our motto—but discontinuity was Miss Rheingold's style. Instead of having us work on our papers she showed us a movie.

Discontinuity can have a powerfully disturbing effect on the young mind, as a simple experiment demonstrates. (Caution: This experiment can be dangerous. For one thing, Step 1 can get you into some trouble, so it's a good idea to prepare in advance a little speech on the value of science education and the experimental method.) You will need a candle, some fine white flour, a sharp knife, a metal punch or tin snips, a garden hose or other long rubber tube, and a large can with a lid. The best type of can is one in which potato chips are sold to institutions, such as the Purlieu Street School.

1. Use the knife to cut the fitting from one end of the garden hose.
2. With the tin snips or metal punch, make a hole in the side of the can, as close as possible to the bottom, just large enough to allow you to insert the end of the hose that no longer has a fitting. Extend the hose an inch or two into the can.
3. Light the candle, and use dripping candle wax to seal the hose in the hole. Extend the hose to its full length, placing

its other end as far from the can as possible. This step is important. You will be at that end of the hose. Read on, and you will soon understand why you want your end to be as far from the can as possible.

4. Inside the can, drip some more wax onto the bottom, roughly opposite the hose. Blow the candle out, and stand it in its own drippings. Hold it in position until it is firmly seated.

5. Put a handful of flour just in front of the hose opening and shape it into a nice little conical heap.

6. Light the candle and place the lid on the can. Do not press it into place tightly; just rest it on top of the can, but without leaving gaps. (See Figure 3.)

7. Walk to the far end of the hose, take a deep breath, and blow into the hose as suddenly and forcefully as you can.

If you have followed these directions carefully, your puff of breath will scatter the cone of flour into a zillion minuscule particles discontinuously distributed in the air within the can, the candle flame will ignite the first few particles that come within its range, the heat of their sudden ignition will ignite others, and so on, and before you can say, *"Now* I see the unsettling effect discontinuity can have on a kid," the can will flip its lid with a rewarding *foom!*

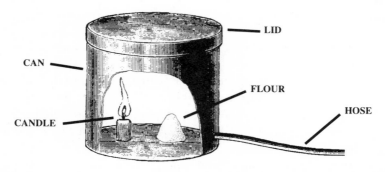

Figure 3: Cutaway view of apparatus to demonstrate the effect of discontinuity.

12

THE MOVIE Miss Rheingold showed us was called *Quanto the Minimum.* It was developed, or at least sponsored, by the telephone company, and it featured a tiny cartoon character, Quanto the Minimum himself, who explored the constitution of matter as it was then understood. Try as I might, I've been unable to scare up a copy of this film to review for this book, so I will have to rely on memory to summarize it for you.

As I recall, Quanto was an impish sort, sarcastic and even a bit nasty. He seemed always to be telling us, the captive audience, how stupid or ignorant we were. This abuse started right off the bat, when Quanto stood with his little hands on his cartoon hips and said right at us, "Hey, kids, I'll bet you think you're really something, don't you? Ya-ha-ha! Well, get this—you're really mostly nothing! Just wait till I get through here. You'll find out that you're mostly empty space. Ya-ha-ha! Come on! Come on along with me! I'll take you on a remarkable voyage of discovery—from the farthest reaches of the universe to the tiniest heart of the tiniest atom—from the vastness of your ignorance to the tiniest little twinkling photon of enlightenment, which is really about all I can realistically expect to pass on to you with the budget they've given me to work with. So hang on! You're in for some surprises. You're about to find out that most of everything is nothing."

Quanto did take us on a remarkable voyage, as he promised, but he was a difficult guide to follow because his style, like Miss Rheingold's, was discontinuity. He jumped from one topic to another with no more transition than saying, "Wow! That was really something. Aren't you excited? I am. I'm really excited!" Then,

foom, off he'd go. He seemed to whiz right off the screen and rock-
et through a radioactive blue miasma for a couple of seconds, eventually reappearing in another location, calmer, a little worn out,
breathing heavily, his snazzy red outfit torn here and there, to tackle
the next topic. "Whew!" he might say. "That was quite a ride.
Where are we? Ah! Alamogordo. Wait till you see this."

We saw many things, a fascinating jumble: an atomic bomb blast
flipping battleships like toys in a tub, solar flares lashing out like
the whip my favorite movie cowboy carried, a Tinkertoy lattice that
represented the molecular structure of some crystal or other and
made chemistry look like lots of fun, and more. We learned a word
that all of us went around using whenever we got half a chance
since it was such a pleasure to say. It began with a funny buzzing,
hissing, and shushing, generated a lot of saliva along the way, and
its ultimate syllable made my mouth a cavernous space in which a
howl resounded. This wonderful word was *Zwischenraum*, the
word Quanto used for the empty space that is most of everything,
the nothing that permeates and separates it all. I now had quite an
incantation: *Zwischenraum, shandy, ontology, epistemology, bills
of lading, splines.*

Among all the marvels in *Quanto the Minimum*, however, the
universal favorite was a demonstration of the mousetrap model of a
fission reaction. In this demonstration, a Ping-Pong table was covered with mousetraps, densely packed, but set at angles to one another, so that the model wouldn't seem to be regularizing matter
too artificially. All of the mousetraps were cocked and ready to
spring, and resting on the wire bail of each was a Ping-Pong ball.
An announcer appeared at the side of the Ping-Pong table. Quanto
leaped onto the screen, said, "Keep your eye on this guy," and
leaped off, laughing.

The announcer waved his hand toward the Ping-Pong table, taking in its entire magnificent array of cocked traps and ready balls,
and said in defiance of all logic, "*This* is Uranium 235."

Then he went on to explain some things he seemed no clearer
about than we were. He seemed to keep losing the distinction between the Ping-Pong ball he was holding as the Ping-Pong ball it
actually was and the neutron it was meant to represent. Whenever

he said that a neutron was used to bombard the Uranium 235 he made a dart-throwing motion with his hand, suggesting that the bombarding process was a heck of a lot like dart throwing, or at least that was the impression it left on most of us. When he had finished his taxing explanation, he said, "And *this* is the result," and with coy insouciance tossed the ball into the array of traps.

Wow.

What resulted may or may not have been a good demonstration of what occurs during nuclear fission, but I am certain that I will never see a more vivid demonstration of an idea that my parents had tried to hammer into me back when I was just a kid, before I took up junk browsing as a pastime, whenever I became bored on rainy vacation days and pleaded with them to mitigate my boredom with a new model airplane kit or a dozen comic books. What they said—and this Ping-Pong ball experiment so spectacularly proved—was, "You don't need model kits and comics to have fun. You can have a lot of fun with the things you find around the house if you just use a little imagination." Definitely so, provided you could find a few dozen mousetraps and Ping-Pong balls.

The film ended. The fluorescent lights stuttered and flickered into life.

"We just have time for a few questions," said Miss Rheingold.

Hands shot up all over the room. Miss Rheingold beamed with pleasure and satisfaction.

"Yes, Spike," she said.

"How do they get those Ping-Pong balls to stay on the mousetraps like that?" She was poised to take notes.

"I—I don't really know," said Miss Rheingold. "Um, Peter?"

"Do you think a little piece of tape would do it?" I asked. "If you curled it around and stuck it back on itself, the way you do when you want to stick something up on the wall without using a tack?"

"I guess it would," said Miss Rheingold. "But that's not really what—"

"Rubber cement," called Dave Botsch, from the back of the room. These were the first words I'd ever heard the overgrown thug volunteer in a classroom in the seven years that he'd been attending school with me. Even his highly persuasive arguments about the wisdom of my giving him portions of my lunch were mostly nonverbal. "You can steal it from the supply closet in the art room," he elaborated. "First cabinet on the left. One little drop on each ball. Let it dry a little, so it's just tacky. Then set it in place. Carefully." With that he lapsed again into his accustomed silence and did not break it again from that day to the day he quit school nearly four years later, when he said something that I remember as "Yaaaaahhhh!"

"Well—" said Miss Rheingold. "And you, Bill?"

"Can you use just regular mousetraps, or do you have to get that model 235 they were using there in the movie?"

It took Miss Rheingold a moment to recognize what a depth of misunderstanding underlay this question. When she did, her shoulders and the corners of her mouth dropped simultaneously. "Oh," she said, or perhaps she just moaned. The bell rang.

We hear from time to time about the power of an idea to influence people, as individuals and in the mass. Usually it's politicians, religious fanatics, or pop philosophers who expect to use ideas to whip people into line, but the most powerful idea I've ever encountered had nothing to do with phony promises, false gods, or bogus ontologies. It was that table covered with mousetraps and Ping-Pong balls. Now *that* was a powerful idea! I would guess that, at minimum, 95 percent of the students in Miss Rheingold's class walked out of the Purlieu Street School that afternoon with the firm determination to make whatever sacrifice might be necessary to acquire a Ping-Pong table and a couple of dozen mousetraps and balls, and recreate the experiment we'd seen in *Quanto the Minimum.* I know that most of us didn't actually do it, but that isn't surprising. In time the task must have come to seem too hard, or much less important than other tasks that came along, or even just plain silly. It takes a special mind to stick to a determination to do something just for the hell of it, the kind of mind my great-great-grandfather Black Jacques Leroy had and few others do.

I wanted to ask one more question before I left, so I stopped at Miss Rheingold's desk, where she sat on the edge watching the class converge on the door, pass through it, and expand into the hall. "Venturi," she muttered.

"Miss Rheingold?" I said.

She pressed a hand to her honeydew brow. "Peter," she said. "I hope this isn't another question about mousetraps."

"No," I said. "Oh, no." Actually, I had wanted to ask if the traps had to be aligned precisely as those in the film had been and, if so, whether it might be possible for me to come back after school and see *Quanto the Minimum* again so I could memorize the arrangement, but I could tell from the way she ran her fingers through her shandy hair that for some reason Miss Rheingold didn't want to talk about mousetraps, and I certainly didn't want to annoy her, so I said, "No, no. It's about my question, 'Where do you stop?' I tried to find the answer in the library, but they don't have any books there that have anything about it. All their books are kind of simple."

She smiled. I was pleased to have caused it.

"I think I can help you," she said.

The smile that came to her lips, the twinkle that came to her eye told me that my discovery that the library's books were too simple for the Big Questions had all been part of her plan for me. I was *supposed* to discover that the question took me beyond the obvious sources. I was supposed to come to her, or to go elsewhere, but in any event to expand my horizons. I must be getting somewhere, I reasoned. She went to the storeroom and returned with a book even thicker and heavier than our general science text.

"Try this," she said.

It was called *Elementary Introductory Physics Made Easy for Beginners (Book One)*. I tried to read it. I really did. My problem was that I understood only a portion of what I read, and the portion I understood was not the portion that conveyed most of the meaning. I moved my eyes along the sentences, did my best to pronounce the words, and used my dictionary quite a lot, but so much of what I read was incomprehensible to me that, in a way, my reading brought me closer to my father, because for the first time I really understood what he meant when he said, as he often did, "It's Greek to me." Here is a passage from the book as it appeared to me then, which is exactly the way I still recall it:

The "χορρεσπονδενχε πρινχιπλε" attempts to define the ρελατιονσηιπ between the μαχροσχοπιχ or "everyday" ρεαλμ (where χλασσιχαλ πηψσιχσ οβταινσ, the δομιναντ force is gravity, and we can believe most of what our senses tell us) and the μιχροσχοπιχ ρεαλμ at ατομιχ or συβατομιχ scales (where θυαντυμ πηψσιχσ οβταινσ, the δομιναντ forces are ελεχτρομαγνετισμ and the strong and weak ιντεραχτιονσ, and Heisenberg's υνχερταιντψ πρινχιπλε describes the limits of what we can know).

It resembles coleslaw: discontinuous but recognizable shreds of cabbage in an indescribably complex entanglement, with an opaque sauce that almost fills the *Zwischenraum*. Remarkably, I managed to derive two ideas from the first chapter. They were these:

1. Things get very much more difficult to understand as you get very much closer to them.
2. As Quanto said, "Most of everything is nothing."

13

WHEN THE GROUPS MET for the first time, a couple of days later, Miss Rheingold told us to spend the period discussing our questions. We didn't have to come to any particular decisions at this first session, she explained. All we had to do was "make a start." When those of us who had figured out that we were in the where-do-you-stop group brought our chairs into a circle around a table, we saw that we were only three. That couldn't be right. Miss Rheingold had said that there would be four people in each group. The fourth member had to be one of the black kids. We waited, twisting on our chairs and looking around for whoever it might be, and in a moment he made his way over to us, holding his slip of paper, extending it the way we held our tickets out for the cranky man who barred the door at the Babbington Theatre at the Saturday matinees.

"'Where do you stop?'?" he asked.

"Yes," I said. We introduced ourselves. His name was Marvin Jones. The other members of our group were Matthew Barber and Patricia Fiorenza. I was amazed to find that at some point during the summer Patricia had developed breasts and begun calling herself Patti—or, for all I knew, the other way around.

I felt that my combat with *Elementary Introductory Physics* qualified me to be the leader of the group, and no one bothered to oppose me. However, the first crisis of my administration occurred immediately following my election, when Nicky Furman, another of the spectacularly overgrown thugs who had sprung up in the summer between sixth and seventh grades, arrived at our table and announced that he was going to join us.

"I was in the what's-the-biggest-question-of-all group, but it wasn't the right group for me," he said. He grabbed a chair, shoved Matthew Barber's chair to one side, though Matthew was in it, and insinuated his chair between Matthew's and the lucky one that held the newly curvaceous Patti.

"Why, Nicky?" asked Patti, poking her lower lip out lusciously.

"The question wasn't big enough," muttered Matthew.

"Let me tell you something," Nicky said. He leaned in toward the center of the table, and the rest of us copied him. "Everybody in that other group is stupid."

This brought a snort from Matthew, which Nicky disapproved.

"Hey, don't make fun of them," he said. "What can they do about it, you know? They're dumb—that's that. It's not really their fault. They're born dumb, they're always going to be dumb. Too bad, but what can you do? We've all got our limitations, right? Even me and you, Barber. Especially you. So anyway I'm sitting there in the what's-the-biggest-question-of-all group, and I look around and I see everybody in the group is stupid. Pow! It hits me. I say to myself, 'These guys are stupid, *therefore* they're going to get the wrong answer to this question. Where is that going to leave me? I know *I'm* not going to do any of the work. I'm going to leave it up to them, right? The answer they get is going to be wrong—not only wrong but *dumb*. I'm going to flunk. I'm at the mercy of fools!' Then I say to myself, 'I need to be in a group of smart guys, 'cause they're going to get the right answer, whatever the question is.' So I look around the room and I see that this is the smart group. Everybody in this group looks smart, you know?"

He turned toward Patti and took her little chin in his hand.

"Except you," he said. "You look gorgeous."

"Gee, thanks, Nicky," said Patti.

Nicky turned toward me and rolled his eyes. "So I say to Miss Rheingold, 'Can we answer a question with a question?'

"And she says, 'Only if you answer the question that you use to answer the question.'

"So I say, 'What question are those guys working on?' Meaning you guys.

"And she says, 'Is that your answer?'

"And I say, 'No, no. That's just a preliminary question, leading to my answer.'

"So she says, 'Where do you stop?'

"And I say, 'I think that's the answer to this question.'

"And so she says, 'Very clever, Nicky. Very clever.' You like that, Barber? 'Very clever.' And then she says, 'Go ahead and join that group if they have no objections.' So here I am."

He looked around the table slowly.

"And I know you don't have any objections, right?" he said.

I wanted to be a strong leader, but I was scared to death of Nicky Furman. I didn't want anyone, especially Patti, to know that, so, trying mightily to give the impression that the question of Nicky's joining our group was of no interest to me whatsoever, I said, "I think the important thing is that we should get right to work. Everybody agree?"

There were silent nods from everyone.

"Okay," I said. "I've been doing some reading, and here's what I've got so far. Everything we see, everything in the world—well, in fact, everything in space and everywhere—is made up of smaller parts. Everybody knows that from the movie, right?"

"Sure," said Matthew, "smaller and smaller parts."

"Okay," I said.

"And Barber's parts are the smallest in the room," said Nicky.

Matthew ignored this remark, other than rolling his eyes toward the ceiling, and I tried to ignore it too.

"Well, the smallest parts are atoms, right?" I said.

"The smallest in the *school*," said Nicky.

"Except for the *parts* of atoms," I continued. "Like the nucleus and the electrons."

"Barber's parts are so small they're *atomic*," said Nicky.

Matthew just sat there, staunchly ignoring Nicky.

"Here's an idea I had," said Marvin. He immediately got our attention, since none of the rest of us knew what he was like, what he thought or felt, what he might have to say, and we had all, without realizing it, been sitting in anticipation of the first time he would open his mouth. Even Nicky was interested. He turned from Matthew to see what Marvin had to say. "Remember what Quanto

said," said Marvin. "Most of an atom is empty space, and everything is made of atoms, so most of *us* is empty space too."

"Barber's head is all empty space," said Nicky, but even he must
have felt that his interruption of Marvin wasn't welcome, because
he spoke in an oddly subdued way.

"If most of us is empty space," said Marvin, "then something
small enough could travel through that empty space." He paused,
and in the pause he turned toward Nicky, just barely turned. It was
so slight a movement that no one could have accused him of deliberately addressing his next remark to Nicky. Then he said, "It
could go right through you."

I looked around the table. Judging from the looks, Marvin had
struck a nerve.

"You mean something could be going through me right now?"
asked Nicky. He put his hand on his stomach, then looked down
and slowly pulled his hand away, as if he expected to see blood.

"Could be," said Marvin. "You know, there are tiny little mete-
orites falling out of the sky all the time."

Nicky's mouth twitched, and the skin under his eyes puckered.
He glanced upward. For the first time in my experience, he looked
vulnerable.

"And then there are rays," said Marvin, with a resigned shrug, as
if to say that it was a shame we were doomed to death by rays but
there wasn't anything any of us could do about it but live our lives
and hope to be missed for a few more years.

Nicky swallowed hard.

"X rays," said Marvin. "Gamma rays. Cosmic rays."

Nicky pressed his hand against his stomach again. Matthew
wore a small smile.

"But that's beside the point," said Marvin. "I just wanted to say
that there's a lot of empty space in us—"

"Right," I said. "And there's a lot of empty space *outside* us—"

Marvin smiled at me, then turned back toward Nicky. "So some
of the empty space in you"—he nodded at Nicky—"could be mixed
up with the empty space outside of you."

"It's hard to tell where you stop, see?" I said.

"What the fuck are they talking about?" asked Nicky, looking

around the group. It was obvious to everyone, I think, that he'd
been shaken. He was still holding his hand to his stomach, for one
thing, and his voice had none of the old edge.

"Do you have to say that?" asked Matthew.

"Fuck you," said Nicky.

"Oh, very good," said Matthew.

"How would you like your face punched, Barber?" asked Nicky,
as if he were offering to do Matthew a favor. "We'll conduct a little
experiment to see where my fist stops and your face starts."

"Ah! Now we're getting somewhere," said Patti.

"We are?" said Matthew.

"Yes," said Patti. "I think Nicky and Marvin have put us on the
right road." She consulted a page in her ring binder. She had been
taking notes. "Marvin has suggested the theoretical underpinning,"
she said. Chewing and snapping her gum, she looked around the
group to see if we agreed. We must not have been wearing satisfactory expressions, because she said, to explain her position, "I think
that business about the space that's in something and the space
that's not in it is really what we ought to be thinking about. I
mean," she said putting her thumb and forefinger to her mouth and
with her tongue pushing her wad of pink gum between them,
"who's to say where my *Zwischenraum* stops and the *Zwischenraum* in this gum starts, you know?" She popped the gum back into
her mouth and resumed chewing and snapping it. "And Nicky did
his part. He came up with an idea for an experiment."

Nicky clenched his fist and grinned.

"Of course, he was only kidding about punching Matthew," she
said. "Weren't you, you big jerk?" The way she said "big jerk"
was so full of promise that I would have been delighted to hear it
applied to me.

"If you punched Matthew," she said, "and we looked at it as
closely as Quanto the Minimum looked at everything, we really
might wonder where your fist stopped and Matthew's face started.
I think we should work on that. You were only kidding, of course,
Nicky, but we could take off from your idea and come up with
some experiments that we might really be able to do."

"Glad I could help," said Nicky. "We made a start, right?"

"Right," said Patti.

"You know what that means," said Nicky.

"What?" asked Marvin.

"That means we can knock off," said Nicky.

He was right. We were only required to make a start. Once we had done that, we could knock off, so, with unanimous relief, we did.

14

IN THE HALL, I threw myself into the usual chaos of kids hurrying for their lockers before catching their buses for home, bumping against one another, rebounding, bumping into someone else, bouncing with a Brownian shuffle. Every time I found myself in this mad shuffle, the experience made me want to change the combinations on the locks—and that made me giggle, with the result that every time I changed classes I giggled like a zany. Someone grabbed my sleeve. It was Matthew.

"What's so funny?" he asked.

"Oh, nothing," I said. "Nothing."

"Peter," he said, "you're becoming very strange. Look, I think we have to have a talk."

"Okay," I said.

"Before this gets out of hand."

"Yeah?"

"I know you mean well, but I have to tell you something."

"What?"

"The group is on the wrong track."

"What do you mean?" This came from behind us. We turned to find Marvin there.

"We're barking up the wrong tree," said Matthew.

"Huh?" said Marvin.

"We're way out in left field," said Matthew.

"I understand what you're saying," said Marvin. "But I don't understand *why* you think we're on the wrong track barking up the wrong tree way out in left field."

"Oh," said Matthew. "Well, I think you've fundamentally misinterpreted the question."

"Thanks," said Marvin.

"You're welcome," said Matthew. "The problem is that you're interpreting it too narrowly."

"Really?" I said.

"Really," said Matthew.

"Is that so?" I said.

Matthew frowned. "You don't have to keep making those little responses to what I say, Peter," he said.

"No?" I said.

"No," he said. "Just be quiet and let me talk."

"Right," I said.

"I've been doing a lot of thinking about this question," he said.

"Well, I've been doing a lot of thinking about it, too," I said.

I *had* been doing a lot of thinking about the question, and I had some good ideas about it. At least they seemed good to me. I liked them. I was very fond of them, in fact. Our affection for our ideas can be as strong as our feelings for people, and it's surprising how quickly our attachment grows. I already felt something like the protective love of a parent for my interpretation of Miss Rheingold's question. Perhaps it was a paltry thing, but it was mine, and hearing it attacked, dismissed, I felt the same kind of sting I would have felt if Matthew had been attacking *me,* my worth, my existence, my merit. This response may have been irrational, but we are rational beings who often behave in irrational ways. Criticisms of our ideas, our words, our work feel like criticisms of our selves, in toto, not just that part of us that is under attack. Where, after all, do we draw the line between our ideas and our selves?

"I'm sure you have," said Matthew. Our eyes locked for a moment. "However—" He let that hang in the air until I responded.

"Yeah?" I said.

"As I see it, Miss Rheingold asked these questions because she wants us to achieve a synthesis of all the branches of science. You're only thinking about one area of inquiry—physics—but what we're supposed to be learning is called *general* science, remember?"

I was going to say something, but as soon as I opened my mouth, Matthew pointed a silencing finger at me and continued: "So she wants us to answer questions that make us think about all the branches of science in a unified way. There are lots of ways to think about the question, but only one of them ties all the kinds of science together, and I've figured out what it is. You see, the question is really a question about thinking. It's a question about *questions*. The real point of the question is this: *At what point do you stop thinking about the question?* If you think about it, you'll realize I'm right. Haven't you found that you can't stop thinking about the question? You go home after school and you need a break, but you can't stop thinking about it."

"True," said Marvin.

Matthew said, "I couldn't get to sleep at night because I couldn't stop thinking about the question. My mother told me to try thinking about something else, so I did, but whatever I tried thinking about would turn into thinking about the question. Every time."

I understood what he meant. I was having similar difficulties with Miss Rheingold's legs.

"I know what you—" I began.

"Please, Peter," he said. "My mother told me to think about food. Pick one of my favorite meals, she said. Then imagine sitting down to eat it on a cold winter's night. Eat my way through it, bite by bite, she said, and by the time I finished my dessert I'd be asleep. It sounded like pretty good advice to me, so I tried it."

"What did you have?" Marvin asked.

"That's not important," Matthew said.

"But what you imagined eating might be a clue—" I began.

"All right, all right," said Matthew. "Roast beef. Mashed potatoes. Lima beans. Chocolate pudding."

"Lima beans?" Marvin said. "Your mother tells you to imagine one of your favorite meals and you think of lima beans?"

"I started eating," said Matthew, "and I was enjoying myself. I even started feeling a little sleepy."

"Eating a big meal can do that," I said.

"But then I started getting worried," said Matthew. "What if I got down to the bottom of my dish of pudding and I wasn't asleep?"

"Uh-oh," I said.

"So I had seconds," said Matthew. "I went on eating happily for a while, but then the same worry came back again."

"I get the picture," said Marvin.

"I fell asleep finally," said Matthew, "but I'm not sure when. It must have been somewhere in my fourth helping. I was starting to feel a little sick by then. I never want to see roast beef again, I can tell you that."

"Or lima beans," said Marvin.

"Of course, you've probably already guessed that by the time I finally did fall asleep, I wasn't really thinking about the food anymore—I was thinking about *the question.* I realized that I was wondering where being awake stops and being asleep starts. Even worse, I was thinking about where thinking about how much roast beef I could eat stops and thinking about where we stop starts. You see what I mean?"

"Yeah," said Marvin and I.

"So," said Matthew, "that's when I realized that the point of the question is where—or when—do you stop thinking about this question. It's a question about how our minds work, how we know what we know—"

"Epistemology," said Marvin.

"—and what there is for us to know in the first place," Matthew continued.

Marvin nodded. "Ontology," he said. I could see that Marvin enjoyed throwing words around as much as I did, and I could tell that we were going to be friends.

"Well," said Matthew. "You see what I mean. It's a question about *everything.*"

"Couldn't we split the question up?" asked Marvin. "Each of us take part of it?"

"That's a fine idea," said Matthew. "You two work on the obvious part. I'll work on the *big* question, the whole synthesis. When we put the report together, your answer can go in as one of the chapters. That'll be fine."

"What about Nicky and Patti?" I asked.

"Those two?" He sneered and said, "They can draw the cover." He walked off. About halfway down the hall he stopped at his locker, spun the dial twice to the right, stopped at the first number, twisted it leftward to the second number, then rightward to the third, and lifted the latch. Since no one had changed the combination yet, the door swung open easily.

I LOOKED AT MARVIN for a moment and then asked him the question that had been in the back of my mind since the first day of school: "Marvin," I asked, "where do you live?"

He grinned. "Is that another of the Big Questions?" he asked.

I shrugged and shook my head, because at that time I didn't realize that it was.

15

MARVIN LIVED in the northernmost section of Babbington, the section called Scrub Oaks, an area I had never seen before. I rode there on my bicycle, a Shackleton Superba.

It was a red bicycle with white pinstripes. The tires were wide and plump, and broad fenders covered them front and rear. Mounted on the front fender was a light, roughly the shape of the fuselage of an airplane. A chrome visor above the lens wrapped over each side of the housing and swept backward, diminishing into two chrome strips that ran along the sides and then broadened again at the rear to form flattened, stylized versions of a plane's ailerons. A small key, the only key I owned, could be inserted into the rear of the light housing to unlock it and allow the top half to be flipped aside for easy access to the batteries, and frequent access was necessary, because the batteries of my youth leaked. Over the rear fender there was a rack, heavily chromed. The handlebars were fitted with red rubber handle grips, with circular protectors just ahead of them, like those I saw on cutlasses in swashbuckling movies, which I still enjoyed though they were already out of date and corny.

Of all the Superba's features, the one that most enchanted me, the one thing that, when I began hinting, pleading, whining, and begging for a full-sized bike, made it not merely *a* bike that I hinted, pleaded, whined, and begged for, but *this* bike, the magnificent Superba, was its horn. It was fitted into the space between the double bars of the frame that arched gracefully from the front fork to the post that supported the seat. Lesser models had nothing in this space but *Zwischenraum*, but I'd never perceived the space as empty until I'd seen, on the Superba, how gloriously it could be filled. Fitted between the bars was a metal box modeled after the gas tank of a motorcycle. On the right side was a circular button with a convex surface to accommodate a fingerpad, and on the left was a chrome grille, behind which was the horn itself. The same key that unlocked the light housing unlocked the horn housing, allowing easy replacement of *its* leaking batteries.

When I first got my Superba, I was much too small to ride it properly. I couldn't reach the pedals. My father bolted blocks of wood onto either side of each pedal. These blocks allowed me to ride the bike, but I still couldn't mount it in the normal manner. I had to bring it to the front steps of our stoop, hold it while I mounted the steps to the top of the stoop, climb aboard while steadying the bike with a hand on the stoop, then start myself with a mighty shove so that I'd clear the stoop before I began to pedal. The blocks gave each pedal the approximate dimensions of a brick, and having two bricks pumping up and down close to the road beneath me made sharp turns an unpredictable affair. If, when I made a turn, leaning into it, racer style, the inside pedal was down, the block bolted to it was likely to strike the pavement and, acting simultaneously as brake and pivot, create some heart-stopping unintentional maneuvers. In the first year, I rarely rode far from home while the blocks were still on, primarily because of the embarrassment of having to remount under unfamiliar conditions, but also because the hazardous blocks made it seem wise to stay close to a sure supply of Band-Aids, mercurochrome, and motherly comfort. When I had finally grown enough so that the blocks could came off, my world (by which I mean the world that I could explore on my own, independent of my parents, who often seemed to hustle me past the most interesting sights) enlarged with the thrilling, dizzying suddenness of one of Quanto's amazing leaps. That bicycle opened all of Babbington to me. Without it, I would never have gone as far from home as Marvin's house, but thanks to my Superba not even Scrub Oaks was outside my range.

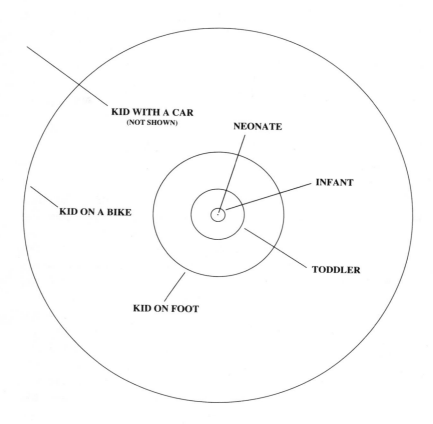

Figure 4: Concentric rings show the roughly logarithmic expansion of a person's range with age, beginning with the newborn's barred crib (though we might just as well have begun in the womb); then the infant crawling on hands and knees; the toddler lurching about from room to room or across a lawn, chasing kittens; the preadolescent child (or "kid") on foot; the growing child on a bicycle ("kid on a bike"); and the vastly greater range, too great to show on this diagram, of an adolescent with a driver's license and an automobile, even if the automobile has to be back in the family garage before midnight ("kid with a car"). Much too large to show on this scale, of course, are the limits of an adult with a credit card (the globe), of human beings (the orbit of the moon, so far), human artifacts (just beyond the solar system, so far), and human-produced radiation (let's say a million light years, counting the radiating photons from the first campfire of homo erectus).

16

FOR THE FIRST SEVERAL BLOCKS of my ride to Marvin's, what I saw was familiar, but then I crossed a narrow concrete road and found myself in territory previously unknown to me. The road cut across the grid of streets and avenues at an angle. It was made of rectangular concrete segments joined, or separated, by seams of tar that projected upward a bit above the concrete and made my Superba's tires thumpa-thump every ten feet or so.

Between the two sides of this road, there was a clear and evident difference. On the northern side there were no tall trees, just some of the scrub oak that had given the place its name and some stunted pine trees with skinny limbs and ragged needles, not much more than shrubs. The housing blocks were rectangular, arranged in a regular grid. There were no exceptions to this grid beyond the slanting line of the concrete road that marked its edge. The houses were similar, and the yards around them were small.

The streets were numbered, not named. This was remarkable to me. I knew that streets in cities were numbered, or at least that some were. I think I had the idea that the streets in cities were numbered because there were too many to name. One could run out of suitable names for streets pretty quickly, but, as Miss Rheingold had pointed out, there was no end of numbers. In the parts of Babbington I knew, the streets had names, and even I was aware of the way their names individualized them. History and anecdotes hovered around them. An aura emanated from their signposts, the invisible equivalent of the comforting aureole surrounding street lamps on a misty night. Everything in the Babbington I knew radi-

ated its past like that. There seemed to be no past to these numbered streets or, by extension, to the whole of Scrub Oaks.

How many dogs did I see? I have a memory of a dog at every
house, barking dogs on long tethers. There were no sidewalks. The
edges of the yards just sloped into the road. The streets were narrow, paved with tar, and badly paved at that, rippled with little
thank-you-ma'ams over which I bounced. I enjoyed that. I remember small children, too young for school, leaning against mailboxes,
door frames, fences, and parked cars, one sucking his thumb, another chewing a bit of her dress, another eating a banana, watching
with shy eyes while I passed on my Superba. All of these children
were black—I would have said "Negro" then—and the fact that
they were all black struck me as remarkable and puzzling, but the
thought never occurred to me that I was as remarkable and puzzling
to them.

There was a swing set in the front yard at Marvin's house; he'd
used it as an identifying feature when he gave me directions. There
was a Studebaker in the driveway—a four-year-old Champion two-
door sedan. Had they bought it at Babbington Studebaker? They
must have. Did Guppa know the Joneses, then? Had he sold their
car to them? Had he been here? I used to help Guppa with the
research for his Studebaker selling, sometimes filling out the cards
he kept on prospects. He considered everyone a prospect. There
were many cards for Joneses. Had I filled out a card for Marvin's
family?

I walked my Superba up the driveway, put the kickstand down,
and went to the front door. Something good was cooking. I wasn't
sure what, but it smelled good, and it made me hungry.

17

MY FIRST IMPRESSIONS of Marvin's family were of bustle and plumpness. There was a lot going on at Marvin's house. He had two younger siblings, a sister and a brother, and they provided running, hopping, tussling, crawling, squealing, and giggling enough for many more children than two. Marvin's mother was rushing around in the kitchen, making the clatter that arose from making dinner, humming and singing while she worked, calling out to the children in what seemed to be a foreign language, laughing at nearly everything Marvin said.

"Mom," he said, "this is Peter." She laughed. "I know him from school," said Marvin, and she laughed again. "He's in my group in science."

"Peter," she said to me. "Peter what?" She laughed again.

"Peter Leroy," I said, and I laughed. She made it seem the thing to do.

"Leroy," she said. "*Le roi.*"

I heard it as ler-wah. I didn't know what she meant by it, so I laughed again.

"The king," she said.

"Heh-heh-heh," said I.

"Are you French?" she asked.

"Um, no," I said. "American."

She laughed again, and I didn't have any idea why, but it seemed polite to join her, so I did.

"He's a funny guy, this King Peter," she said to Marvin. She would call me that, off and on, for all the years she knew me.

Later I learned that Marvin's mother was from New Orleans. His father had been a railway mail clerk when he was a young man, traveling in mail cars from North to South and back again, sorting the mail as he rolled along. He had carried a letter of introduction to her family for months but shyness had kept him from using it until, driven by loneliness during a layover, he had at last come to call and fall in love. They—but all that is another story, and I knew none of it at the time.

My impression of bustle was amplified by the fact that I was working so hard at taking it all in, my eyes darting here and there, my senses working overtime. So much was new to me. On my later visits to Marvin's I noticed none of this bustle. All seemed calm. We tend to see disorder in the unfamiliar—and to discover in it an underlying order only as the unfamiliar becomes familiar.

The plumpness I sensed wasn't a quality of the Joneses themselves, but of their furniture. It was the same plumpness I felt in my grandparents' houses, in their bulbous sofas and ottomans and comfy chairs. It was comfort without opulence; in fact, a certain permissive shabbiness was essential to it, a shabbiness that allowed you to feel at ease, told you not to worry about breaking things or making a mess. I associate this plump comfort with certain foods too, the ones that are thick or soft or round, like dumplings and stew and biscuits and pudding. Mrs. Jones might have been making some comfortable food like that, but I couldn't have said. Nothing she was making was familiar to me.

I had brought the plans for the lighthouse with me, to make a good impression, to show off. I was going to show them off on the living room floor, but when I began spreading them out Marvin suggested we take them upstairs to his room. The aromas of Mrs. Jones's cooking followed us up there.

"What is that?" I asked Marvin. "What's your mother making for dinner?"

"Huh? Oh—court bouillon. Redfish court bouillon."

"What's red fish?"

"It's—I don't know—fish."

"Is it red?"

"No—actually it's white."

"And what's that other part? Say it again?"

"Coobyon. Coo. Byon."

"Coo-be-yon."

"No. Coobyon."

"Coobyon."

"That's it."

"Is that one thing, or are there parts to it?"

He laughed. "One thing. Oh—I see what you mean. It starts out with parts, of course, when she's making it. But when it's done, it's one thing. I mean, you wouldn't be eating court bouillon if you just ate the fish. You have to eat it all. You eat it with rice, too. But that's separate."

"But you always have it? The rice?"

"Yeah."

"Now *that's* interesting," I said. "Something with parts that aren't together—and aren't the same—with *Zwischenraum* in between."

"Yes, it *is* interesting," said Marvin.

"I wonder if we should put that in?" I asked, though I was a little reluctant to give us more work.

I took a deep sniff. It smelled great—strange, but yummy. I didn't have the nerve to ask to taste it, but I sure wanted to.

"Do you eat anything called splines?" I asked, but Marvin's attention was elsewhere. He had unrolled the plans.

"Hey, this is terrific," he said.

"Thanks," I said. "I'm pretty proud of it, I have to admit. I'll tell you something funny about it, though. I have this friend—Raskol—and he thinks that—"

"It's just like those prison movies!" said Marvin, with that instantaneous conviction, immediately unshakable, that we see in people when they embrace mistaken ideas. "You know—where the guy's been convicted for something he didn't do and he has to get out so he can prove that he's innocent, and the girl gets a car for the getaway and she's waiting outside the wall and he's been digging a tunnel for years and finally he crawls through it and comes out in the prison yard but he still has to make a run for it and go over the wall. They always have these watchtowers," he said, indicating my lighthouse. "With a big searchlight turning on the top."

"Yeah," I said.

"And the guy has to dodge the beam when it sweeps past him."

"Right," I said.

There was an explosion of sound from downstairs—whoops and hollers and thundering feet.

"Hey! My father's home," said Marvin. He ran downstairs, and I followed.

Mr. Jones was a surprise. He was small and seemed much older than his wife. The greeting the family gave him was loud and physical. The Joneses hugged, tickled, teased, punched one another's arms, and shouted and squealed an indecipherable mix of mysterious words. It embarrassed me. It seemed like something I shouldn't watch. I didn't know where to look.

"Say, Marvin," said Mr. Jones suddenly. "Who's your friend?"

"This is Peter," said Marvin.

"Peter Ler-wah," said Mrs. Jones. "The king!" She made a little curtsy. "But he calls himself Leroy, because he's not French. He's American."

"Hello there, Peter," said Mr. Jones. To Marvin he said, "Did you show him the chickens?"

"No," said Marvin, pulling a face.

"You didn't show him the chickens?" exclaimed Mr. Jones.

"I don't think he wants to see the chickens," said Marvin.

"Sure he does!" said Mr. Jones. "Peter, if I told you that the world's most amazing chickens were living right in our back yard, you'd want to see them, wouldn't you?"

"You bet," I said. Generally, I didn't care for chickens. The fad of raising and training them had affected most of the fathers in the part of Babbington where I lived. Perhaps they saw it as a way of distinguishing themselves from their fellow fathers in nearly identical houses. They might live matching lives, but they could have the best-bred, best-trained homing flock in the neighborhood. The men generally taught their flocks to respond to whistle signals based on the swing tunes of their heyday, but because they didn't get home until evening and tended to get right down to their beer then, they didn't always have time for the day-to-day practice that kept a homing flock sharp, so that job fell to their children, and the weekday evenings in my neighborhood were full of whistling kids, commanding their fathers' chickens to walk around the block to "Sing, Sing, Sing" or "Pennsylvania 6-5000." It was a great relief to me when my mother declared one evening, the moment my father walked through the back door, "I've had it with those chickens! The dumb clucks are driving me crazy! Either they go or I go!" It was, of course, an even greater relief when the chickens went and my mother stayed. I thought the whole chicken fad was embarrassing, but I had learned that adults had their enthusiasms and thought their children should share them; whether it was two weeks in a tent on a rainy mountainside or swing music or chickens, it was polite to pretend an interest, so I said again, "You bet," and added, "Sure I would!"

"See that, Marvin?" said Mr. Jones. "Not everybody holds chickens in such low esteem as you do. Let's go."

Behind the house were chicken coops, dozens of them, but these were not the jerry-built coops of scrap lumber and chicken wire one usually saw. They were a set of cubes stacked in a clever and varied way, so that they formed an irregular ziggurat in which each chicken had its own garden apartment, one cubical dwelling per chicken, each with a small yard outside its entrance, on the roof of the cubicle below it, with the exception of the ground-level apartments, which had their little yards on the ground. The structure was a handsome and ambitious thing, but something else caught my eye almost at once. In the yard outside each chicken apartment was something turning and sparkling in the sun—a tiny metal tree. The trunks of these trees were made of strands of twisted wire. As they reached upward, the strands unwound from the thick trunk and stretched outward to form branches. Along the branches, wherever a wire came to an end, a bit of shiny metal scrap was fixed to it so that the metal could turn. In even the gentlest breeze, the bits of metal would spin and catch the light. The chickens were sitting in the doorways of their apartments, just sitting there calmly, each watching its own tree, mesmerized by the coruscating bits of tin spinning in the thin evening light.

I knew what I was seeing. I knew immediately. Here was the secret to a prizewinning appearance on "Fantastic Contraptions."

"Peter, I'll bet you've never seen *trained* chickens before," Mr. Jones began.

"Dad," said Marvin, in a tone that any kid I knew would have recognized immediately as meaning "Don't embarrass me."

"Mr. Jones," I said. "Can I ask you something?"

"I'll bet you're wondering if you could train a chicken yourself," he said. "Well, of course you could! It's not easy, don't let anybody tell you that. But it's not impossible. Don't let anybody tell you that, either. You remember what the great Dr. Johnson said about the dangers of overestimating or underestimating a task and how a little work, steadily applied, will eventually achieve its goal."

There was an unspoken "don't you?" at the end of that, and I answered it with "Well—"

"He said that you should carry in your mind, at once, 'the difficulty of excellence, and the force of industry' and remember that 'labor, vigorously continued, has not often failed of its reward.' Now, you take the breeding and training of champion chickens—"

"Actually, Mr. Jones," I said, "what I wanted to know is, did you make those trees?"

"The trees?"

"The little wire trees."

"Why, Mrs. Jones makes those," he said. "Pretty, aren't they?"

"Yes," I said. "They really catch your eye."

"And those windflowers on the ends of the branches—"

"Windflowers," I said. "Yeah, those are something."

"The way they rotate—"

"I like that," I said.

"And scintillate."

"That, too."

"And coruscate."

"Sure."

"Well, the chickens like that, too. It keeps them amused."

"Ah," I said.

"And yet," said Mr. Jones, raising his finger and his tone, "the remarkable thing is that those windflowers keep other birds away. It used to be that when we fed the chickens, the other birds thought we were throwing seed out for everything with wings. They'd come swooping down and take the chickens' dinner before they could eat it. Especially the pigeons. Regular hijackers, those pigeons. When the word got out that we were feeding the chickens, why before you knew it, we'd see the pigeons waiting around for dinner, checking their little watches to see how long it was going to be before we brought it out." He gave me a wink to tell me that the business about the little watches was a joke. "A fellow down the street told me the trick is to have some shiny things hanging on strings so that they flash in the sun—the top of a can, say, or a piece of aluminum foil. That scares the other birds away. So I strung a bunch of junk like that around, and it worked very well—kept the pigeons and the other birds at bay. Not only that, but I noticed that the chickens liked it. They'd stand there gazing at the shiny foil for hours, happy as clams. It mesmerized them. Funny thing, isn't it? The flashing metal frightened the other birds, but amused the chickens. There's probably something very profound behind that discovery, wouldn't you say?"

"I—well—I guess," I said.

Mr. Jones gave me another of those winks of his. "Well," he said, "the can lids worked, but they looked just awful. Marie— Mrs. Jones—couldn't stand it. So she started working on them. She nipped and snipped and clipped at them till she cut them down to size and shaped them into stars and flowers and pinwheels, and eventually this is what came out of it—she makes the metal trees out of scrap wire, and she makes the windflowers—we call them windflowers—for the branches."

Windflowers. *Windflowers, court bouillon, Zwischenraum, shandy, ontology, epistemology, bills of lading, splines.*

"Would you like one?" he asked.

"Oh, no," I said. "No, thanks." It was considered polite at that time to refuse gifts, no matter how much you wanted them.

"You're sure?" said Mr. Jones, reaching for one of the trees.

"No, no," I said. The one he was reaching for wasn't my favorite, so being polite was easier than it would otherwise have been. "Thanks, but—maybe next time."

"Okay," said Mr. Jones. "Marvin, it's time for you to walk the chickens."

"Oh, okay," said Marvin, with a reluctance I recognized. "Want to walk the chickens with me?" he asked.

"Just a little way," I said. "I should be getting back home. I'll walk my bike with you."

"Don't forget your plans," he said.

"Oh, yeah," I said. The three of us walked up the narrow cement steps to the back door and went in through the kitchen. I must have felt that refusing a wire tree with windflowers had built up a pretty good balance in my politeness account, because, although it was also considered impolite to ask for things, I said to Mrs. Jones, "That court bouillon sure smells good. Do you think I could have a taste?"

"For the king," she said, "anything." She ladled a little into a cup, blew on it, and passed it to me. I liked it.

"It's good," I said.

"It's bun soup," she said—for what reason I couldn't begin to imagine—and then she added, with a wink and a smile, "I'll bet you're relieved."

MARVIN AND I walked together for a few blocks, the chickens in two orderly lines ahead of us, Marvin keeping them in line with a few bars from "East St. Louis Toodle-Oo" now and then. He was eager to talk about working on the watchtower, and I tried to appear just as eager as he, but I have a mind inclined to wander, and just then it kept wandering back to the windflowers, the coruscating bits of tin spinning in the thin evening light, just as, at entirely unpredictable times, it would wander to Miss Rheingold's legs or Raskol's sister Ariane or the pleasant anticipation of the day when we would change the combinations of the locks.

18

WHEN I GOT HOME from Marvin's, my father was out on the patio, cooking a chuck steak.

For my father the barbecue season never stopped. There was a period, from November through February, I guess, when conditions kept him from grilling as much as he might have wanted to and when snow sometimes kept him from even reaching the grill, but these were only interruptions of his barbecuing, gaps within a circular season, not the ends of it, so it could never accurately be said of him that he had stopped barbecuing. Does that mean that the barbecue season in Babbington as a whole never stopped? I suppose that for people of a certain elevated social class the season never began—but I'm not at all certain that that could be the case, since it seems to me that on any fine weekend night in the summer the air of Babbington was rich with the odor of burning beef, and if even one griller was at it year round—and my father was that griller—then wouldn't we have to say that the activity itself had no term, that it was a cycle falling from more to less, rising from less to more, seamlessly, endlessly?

My father prided himself on his talent as a barbecue cook. He had built a patio as his outdoor kitchen. It filled the "el" at the back of our house, the space between the projecting dining room and what we called my mother's little room. When our house was originally constructed, its plan was a simple rectangle, but additions had made it more complicated. My father had added a dining room first, straight out the back from the kitchen, and then he had extended the opposite end by adding my mother's little room, which I was told to refer to as a bedroom, though it had no bed and no one slept there. In this room my mother tried for several years to run small businesses of her own, one after another, illegally, I think, since the neighborhood wasn't zoned for that sort of thing. At various times she tried to sell lamps made from bottles encrusted with seashells, chenille automobile seat covers for hot summers, handmade crewel place mats stitched up to resemble photographs of a customer's loved ones, and, as I've mentioned, bamboo fishing poles. The most successful of her businesses, Ella's Lunch Launch, came later—and that is another story. The business that led to the building of her little room was Fudge in a Bunch, fudge molded into the shape of bananas and wrapped in yellow paper that one could peel back bite by bite. My mother launched into the Fudge in a Bunch business with an enthusiasm that completely possessed her. We saw the same captivating enthusiasm at the start of all her other ventures. Each time, she made elaborate plans, designed ads, and made a stab at running whatever business it was, but after a while, when she found it harder and less interesting than she had expected, she began losing interest, the business petered out, its equipment traveled to the cellar, and a new enthusiasm replaced it. It wasn't always easy to tell where one of these enthusiasms stopped and the next began. Each of her businesses left its souvenir. The fishing rods gave us the grove of bamboo, and the fudge bananas gave us my mother's little room. The kitchen became the fudge factory, we wrapped the bananas and assembled the bunches in the dining room, and my father and some friends of his built the little room to serve as the warehouse and executive office suite.

The dining room and my mother's little room altered the shape of the house so that in the back there was a notch where one wall of the dining room met the longer wall of the original house, extended by a wall of my mother's little room. The patio where my father did his barbecuing filled this el. (A nook such as this was always known as "the el" in my neighborhood. I assumed that the name referred to the letter, but research suggests to me that it is derived by extension from an ancient term, *ell* in British English, a shortening of Middle English *ele,* meaning "transept" or "wing," related to *aisle.*)

Most of the homeowners on our block had built patios. Magazines were full of plans for them. In those days people did not have decks. Concrete was the favored patio material in my neighbor-hood. To build a patio, the home handyman began with some boards nailed together to make molds. The concrete mixture was poured into these molds and allowed to harden, and then the result-ing blocks were fitted together on a bed of sand to make the patio. Squares, diamonds, and hexagons were the usual shapes for the blocks, but the man who lived next door apparently found regular polygons dull. He built his patio of unique, oddly shaped blocks, each one molded in place, its shape decided only after a long period of beery meditation. The patio took him months to build, but it must have been worth it, because he was thereafter held in high re-gard as a screwball genius, with depths of personality unimagined before he built his odd patio. My father took a straightforward ap-proach: he built our patio of squares. With such an outstanding ex-ample next door, I found this embarrassing.

"Hey, Peter," said my father, waving the smoke away from his face, "where have you been?"

"I was up in Scrub Oaks," I said.

My mother came out of the house. She had a beer for my father, in the bottle, and a small glass for herself, part of the contents of his bottle.

"Scrub Oaks?" she said. "What were you doing up there?" She was wearing her worried look: a furrowed brow and a frown. I don't remember when this look first appeared, but at about this time she began wearing it more and more.

"I went to see Marvin," I said. "A kid in my science class. He's in the where-do-you-stop group."

"The what?" said my father.

"I told you," I said. "Remember? We have to answer the ques-tion 'Where do you stop?'"

"Who is this Marvin?" asked my mother.

"Marvin Jones. He's a kid in my science class." I must have known what piece of information she was looking for, and knowing what she was looking for must have been what made me withhold it, and that must have been what made me shift the subject. "They don't have any sidewalks up there," I said.

Neither of them said anything. My mother was fussing around

the table. My father was shaking garlic salt onto the steak.

"They don't have any trees, either," I said. "Not real trees, anyway. Just little trees, crummy trees."

"It's the soil," said my father.

"I guess," I said. I knew that this was possible. I had spent
many happy hours testing the soil in our back yard with my grandfather, using a nifty little soil test kit that he had ordered by mail. It
came in a sturdy white cardboard box, inside which were tiny vials
of liquid and larger empty vials. One mixed a pinch of the soil and
some drops of the various liquids in one of the larger vials and then
held the resulting muddy water up to the light of the sun and compared its color with the colors of cellophane circles in a card that
came with the kit. The circles progressed gradually from one color
to another, so gradually that you couldn't say, exactly, where the
dominance of reddish brown ended and the dominance of yellowish
brown began. From this testing I learned that each vegetable requires, in effect, a soil of a different color, so I knew that it might
have been the soil that stunted the trees, but something in my father's voice, a reluctance to continue, said that there was more to it
than that. I had heard this reluctance whenever I raised embarrassing questions. I seemed to hear it more and more, and more and
more it seemed to inspire me to ask embarrassing questions.

"That would account for the trees," I said.

"Sure," said my father.

"But not for the sidewalks."

"Yeah," he said. "Well. That's the way they like it."

I was young, it's true, and I was ignorant, too, but I wasn't stupid, and this explanation was so obviously ridiculous that it opened
the widest crack yet in the myth of my father's good sense. He had
been chipping away at this myth for some time now, but only with
tiny hammers that didn't do much more than surface damage, craz-
ing and nicking it. Now he seemed to have taken up something
heavier, a real sledgehammer, determined to finish off the job.

"It is?" I asked.

"Yes, Peter," he said. "If they didn't like it that way, they'd
change it, wouldn't they?"

"I guess," I said, because I was still a long way away from the time when I would dare to tell him exactly what I thought.

WHEN WE SAT DOWN to eat, my mother wrinkled her nose, leaned over her plate, sniffed at her food, gave it a puzzled look, and asked, "What is that smell?"

"You're right," said my father. "There is something. Was this steak fresh?"

"I thought so," said my mother.

My father raised his plate to his nose and sniffed it. "It's not the meat," he said.

They turned toward me.

"Peter," said my mother, "it's you. What have you gotten into?"

I sniffed my sleeve.

"Oh," I said. "It's coobyon. Redfish coobyon. But Mrs. Jones makes it with flounder, because you can't get redfish around here. It's bun soup." I didn't know exactly what that meant, especially since I hadn't seen any buns in it, but it was what Mrs. Jones had called it, and from tasting it I had gotten the idea that *bun* meant something like "spicy." I'd already added it to my string of favorites: *bun soup, windflowers, court bouillon, Zwischenraum, shandy, ontology, epistemology, bills of lading, splines*—and when I got to *splines* I always thought of changing the combinations of the locks, and, like the look that Flo and Freddie exchanged, that always made me laugh.

"What's so funny?" asked my father.

"Oh, nothing," I said. It was too much to explain, and there were too many parts that were unsuitable for them to hear.

My parents exchanged a look, and we all began eating. I hadn't taken more than a few bites when an impression from my visit to Marvin's struck me so unexpectedly that I blurted it out without thinking about the effect it might have.

"Marvin's house is the same as ours," I said. I was amazed to realize that this was true: the layout of the Jones's house was exactly the same as ours had been when we moved in.

"Don't be ridiculous, Peter," said my father.

I was matching the rooms in my mind. They all fit. The Joneses' house was probably built by the same developer who had built ours and all the others like it on our block, and many others just like it on other blocks in Babbington, using the same set of plans, all of them just alike.

"It's true," I said. "It's true. Their house is exactly like ours."

"It can't be," said my father.

"But it is," I said.

"Do they have a dining room here, where we're sitting?"

"No," I said. "That's not what I meant. I meant the house—"

"And do they have your mother's little room?"

"That's not what I meant."

"You see, Peter? Their house is *not* the same as ours, is it?"

"What I mean is—"

"It's not exactly the same, is it?"

"Look. What I mean is—"

"It's not exactly the same, *is it*?"

"No," I said.

My father laughed and bent to his food. My mother gave a little laugh of agreement, since she had to live with him, but the frown she wore told me that she didn't mean it. I finished eating in silence, and when dinner was done, I went up to my room.

19

"PETER, PETER, PETER," said Porky as soon as I walked through the door of Captain White's. "Your timing is perfect. Sit down, my friend, sit down, sit *down*. We're going to have a taste test."

"Taste test?" I climbed onto a stool at the counter. Porky wiped the spot in front of me with his sleeve.

"Yep," he said. "The Captain's Shandy. I've got to figure out the right ratio of beer to lemonade, and you're going to help me."

"I am?"

"Sure, sure, sure. You're my only investor. Except my father. So you're my favorite investor, anyway."

"I want to tell you something," I said.

"Sure, go ahead. I'm listening."

He wasn't, I thought. There were customers in three or four of the booths, and he kept an eye on them to make sure they were enjoying what they were eating; he poked his head into the kitchen now and then to see how things were going there; and he assembled the necessities for the taste test. I went ahead and told him about my visit to Marvin's anyway, and my parents' reactions to it. Maybe it was easier for me to talk about it when he didn't seem to be listening. In fact, for certain kinds of things that we want to get off our chests, or for things that we want to work through by thinking aloud, the best listener may be one who isn't listening at all but has the good manners to make a listener's grunts from time to time, just enough of a response so that we're encouraged to think that our words, and so our thoughts, are significant. I spoke, on and on, exploring my ideas, while Porky grunted and went on working.

He lined up a number of beer glasses along the counter. He set a

big jug of lemonade at the left end of the line of glasses and a couple of quart bottles of beer at the right.

"Well, Peter," he said, "I'll tell you what it is."

He began pouring lemonade into the glasses. Working from left
to right, he filled the first glass, then poured a little less into the next
glass, a little less into the next, and so on, working his way toward
the right end of the line.

"Your parents are—" he began, and then stopped. "Hey," he said.
"You're not going to get upset if I tell you what I think, are you?"

"No," I said, though it was a promise I wasn't sure I could keep.

"Okay." He had reached the glass nearest the beer bottles. He
left that one empty. "Your parents are participating in a process of
cumulative error."

"Yeah," I said.

"You know what that is?"

"No," I said.

He began filling the glasses with beer, working from right to left.

"Say you're going to build a doghouse."

"Okay."

"You're going to need a whole bunch of boards for the sides, and
of course they all have to be the same length, right?"

"Right."

He added beer to each glass, filling them to the same height,
crouching behind the counter and closing one eye to be sure that
they were even as he worked along the line.

"You measure the first board with a ruler, mark it, and cut it."

"Okay."

"Then, instead of using the ruler for the next board, you just lay
the first one on it and mark the length."

"Yeah."

"Try this," he said. He pushed the leftmost glass toward me, the
one that was all lemonade. I drank some.

"Good," I said.

Porky took a swallow and made a face. "Tastes like lemonade,"
he said. He pushed the next glass toward me. "What happens when
you mark the second board is that the pencil mark is going to be a
little off. You know what I mean?"

"Yeah." I did, from experience. I hoped the source of my understanding didn't show in the way I answered.

Porky pushed another glass toward me. "Hey, don't be embarrassed," he said. "Experience is the best teacher." We sampled the glass. "Still tastes too much like lemonade," he said. "Anyway, you go on to the third board, and instead of using the ruler, you lay the second board down on it, mark it, and cut it, and then you go on marking and cutting the boards like that, each time measuring with the last board you cut, and then when you've got all the lumber cut, you're going to start putting the doghouse together, right?"

"Right."

We moved on to the next glass.

"But nothing fits. The way you measured them, the boards all came out different lengths. You don't have a doghouse. All you've got is a pile of scrap." He took a swallow of shandy. "It's starting to get a little bite to it, don't you think?"

"Maybe," I said.

It *was* beginning to taste a little funny. I didn't have much experience with beer. The swallows I'd had from time to time hadn't persuaded me that it was any better than, say, brussels sprouts.

Porky said, "Well, people are like that, you see. Most of them get their ideas and what they think are facts from the last board down the line. It might be the jerk next door; it might be one of those preachers who are always whining and shouting on the radio; it might be one of those little booklets that hasn't got anybody's name on it."

We had moved a few glasses to the right.

"But you know what they don't do?" Porky asked.

"What?"

It felt kind of interesting to say "What?" The *w* made my lips feel like rubber. I said it again, just for the fun of it. "What?"

Porky raised the next glass in a toast to the wisdom of his next remark. "They never have the good sense to go back to the ruler," he said. I didn't quite get it, but I didn't want Porky to know that, so I took the glass from him, raised it as he had, and drained it off.

"They never go back to the ruler," I said.

"Right," said Porky. "You've got it. They never measure the

things they hear—the dumb ideas in the air around them, the whining of the jerk next door—against their own common sense. They
never check to see if what they're doing still makes any sense. Are
you following me?"

"Oh, sure," I said, taking the next glass Porky passed me and
waggling it to underscore my understanding.

"So, my point is this," said Porky. "Your parents—well, I don't
want you to think I've got anything against them or anything like
that—but they're—" He stopped. "Gee, Peter," he said. "I'm not
sure how to say this to you."

I reached for the next glass on my own. I was pretty sure that
Porky was going to say my parents were full of shit, or something
along those lines, and I didn't want to have to hear him say that. I
didn't want him to have to say it. I didn't want to have to decide
whether I believed it. I decided to beat him to it, say something that
would make it unnecessary for Porky to speak. I didn't know what
I was going to say until I began to talk, but as the words came out of
me I was surprised to find that they were the right ones, and I was
surprised to find how closely I'd been listening to Porky, how well
I'd understood what he'd been saying.

"They're a couple of boards too far down the line," I said.

"That's it, Peter," said Porky.

"Heading toward a pile of scrap."

"Right."

"This *is* getting a nice bite to it," I said, regarding the glass I held
in my hand.

"Yeah, it is," he said, smacking his lips. "But it's not shandy
anymore."

"Huh?"

"This is the end of the line," he pointed out. "It's all beer."

Figure 5: A series of tumblers holding mixtures that progress from lemonade (1) through a succession of shandies to beer (5) also provides a representation of a progression from acidic to basic soil samples in the little vials of a mail-order soil test kit, the range of colors of students in the Purlieu Street School, and the concentrations of Babbingtonians of various shades from Old Babbington Village to Scrub Oaks.

20

I WAS CONVINCED that Guppa and Mrs. Jones would be unbeatable on "Fantastic Contraptions." All they had to do was add some windflowers to one of Guppa's ideas, and they'd have a winner. From my point of view, the work was all but done, the prize all but won, once I brought them together. I knew that Guppa even had a suitable gadget nearly ready. He hadn't said anything to me about it yet, probably because he didn't want me to see something that wasn't perfected, but I'd seen him fiddling around with it in the garden, and sometimes, in the evenings, after he'd gone home to Gumma, I went out and looked it over. It was a device for watering the garden automatically. It got the job done, but that was about all you could say for it.

How my idea of a satisfactory gadget had changed! It wasn't enough any longer to get the intended job done, it also had to get *my* job done: it had to win on "Fantastic Contraptions," and to do that it had to amuse Flo and Freddie and their audience. So far, the watering machine was only halfway there. It consisted of a number of trash-can lids, inverted, suspended from posts at spots in the garden where they would catch water that fell into them, rainwater or water from the lawn sprinklers Guppa had placed here and there. Each lid was hanging from a cord that ran through a set of pulleys to the valve of a toilet tank, which controlled the flow of water to a sprinkler that covered the area of the garden that included that particular trash-can lid. The principle was similar to—but the reverse of—the method that fills a toilet tank to a certain level. In a toilet tank (and you can confirm this in the privacy of your own home), a floating ball rises with the rising water. Through a set of rods and pivots, the ball is linked to a valve. As the ball rises, the valve closes. In Guppa's gadget, the trash-can lid fell as it filled with water and rose as the water in it evaporated. A full lid closed the valve, and a dry one opened it. It was a fine gadget as far as it went. It was effective, but it wasn't attractive or funny.

I wanted so much to just walk right up to Guppa and propose that he and Mrs. Jones collaborate, but I wasn't sure what my opening line ought to be.

This business of opening lines is always problematic, as Guppa himself had often told me. In his line of business—selling Studebakers, that is, not inventing gadgets or farming—it was the first step on the road to success or failure. "The right words lead to a sale," he used to say. "The wrong ones lead out the door." I didn't want to open with the wrong line and see Guppa's chances for victory and fame walk, as it were, out the door, so I fretted a great deal about the opening line, and when you consider the effect of adding my fretting about that to my fretting about my general science paper, you won't be surprised to know that I wasn't sleeping well and bags had begun to form under my eleven-year-old eyes.

MATTERS CAME TO A HEAD on the Saturday afternoon that Raskol and Marvin had persuaded me to set aside for starting work on the lighthouse—that is, the watchtower. They knew I was fretting over the science paper, and they were convinced that building a watchtower would be beneficial.

"It'll take your mind off it," said Raskol.

"And when we're thinking of something else, the answer to the question might just sneak into our minds while we're not looking," said Marvin.

"Hey! I hadn't thought of that," I said.

"I wouldn't count on it," said Raskol.

"Still," said Marvin, "I wouldn't discount it."

"No," said Raskol. Did he wink? "You never can tell."

"Okay," I said. "I'll give it a try."

"Let's start on Saturday," said Raskol.

"Saturday it is," I said.

While I was waiting for them to show up, I dragged lumber from the pile in the garage to the building site atop the hill. Guppa was working in the garden, and I passed him again and again, all the while racking my brain for the right thing to say to lead him into a collaboration with Mrs. Jones, and growing increasingly aware that I ought to say at least *something* to him.

Finally, I stopped on one of my passages and asked, "How's it going, Guppa?" (I don't want you to think that "How's it going, Guppa?" was the best opening line I could come up with for my campaign to get him to collaborate with Mrs. Jones. The campaign hadn't started yet. I was just stalling.)

"Huh?" he grunted, driving his mattock deep into the roots of the bamboo.

"You've really made some progress!" I said.

He *had* made excellent progress. Starting at the back of the garage, where my father had formerly kept his chickens, he had created a rectangular garden plot, advancing toward the back of the yard, the foot of the hill, and the vanguard of the encroaching grove of bamboo. Though the weather was still too cold for Guppa to begin planting the garden, he had already planted a garden in his mind, so there were some shoots of green in there to reward him for his work and keep him at it.

"Thanks," he said. He rested the mattock on the ground, stood up, stretched his back, and pulled his handkerchief from his overalls pocket. "I guess I have at that." He looked back toward the garage and smiled at the green shoots in his mind's garden. "And how about you?" he asked. "How's your science paper coming?"

"I—" I turned away. This wasn't a question I particularly wanted to answer.

"You've been working on it, haven't you?" Guppa asked.

"Oh, sure," I said. "I've been working on it." Thanks to Matthew, I'd come to believe that I was *always* working on it, so I was able to say this with some conviction.

"So," said Guppa, "are you making any progress?"

"It's kind of hard to tell."

"I know what you mean," he said. "Sometimes, you work away at something all day long and when the day is done you just can't tell whether you're any closer to seeing it finished than you were the day before."

"Yeah," I said. "That's exactly the way it is. Sort of like mixing shandy."

"What?" said Guppa.

"You know how, when you're trying to find just the right proportions of beer and lemonade for shandy, you line up some glasses and put a little more beer and a little less lemonade in each one, and the change is so gradual that you hardly know you're changing from one glass to the next?" I said.

"No," said Guppa.

"Oh," I said. He surprised me. I still had the idea that all adults knew the same things, that there was a body of knowledge they shared equally. If Porky knew about shandy, then Guppa, who was so much older, certainly should know about it too. I was embarrassed for him. "Well, it's not important," I said, "but it is kind of like that."

"What's kind of like what?"

"Working on a job and not seeing much progress is kind of like going from one glass to the next—in that shandy business."

"Oh," he said. "I see." He didn't, though.

We stood there for a while. Guppa leaned on the handle of the mattock. I scuffed my shoes in the dirt and wiped my hands on my pants. The unspoken hung in the air around us. One of us had to say something.

"So—" I said.

"Mm?"

"What do you call it?" I knew that he would know what I meant this time.

"Automatic Garden Waterer." Poor Guppa. He hadn't caught on to the Flo and Freddie style. He didn't understand snappiness.

"How about 'The Gardener's Pal'?" I suggested.

"I know what you mean," he said. "'Automatic Garden Waterer' isn't snappy."

"No," I said.

"I did have something else in mind. You might like this. How about 'The Watering Can That Can Water When You Can't'? Get it?"

"It's—um—it's kind of long," I said, imagining Freddie rolling his eyes.

"Hey, Peter! Peter!" Guppa and I turned to see Marvin running across what was left of the lawn. He was holding a piece of cloth and waving it like a flag.

"That's my friend Marvin," I said to Guppa. "Marvin Jones. He's in the where-do-you-stop group with me. He's going to help me build the lighthouse. Watchtower."

"Mm," said Guppa.

"Take a look at this," said Marvin, panting, when he reached us. He handed me what he'd been waving, and I took it.

I examined it and reached a quick conclusion. "It's a dirty rag," I said.

"Right!" said Marvin, beaming. He seemed so delighted and excited by this dirty rag, or, even more than that, by the whole concept of dirty rags, that I was sorry I hadn't paid more attention to them myself.

"Smell it," he said.

I did. "It's kind of sweet-smelling," I said. "I think I recognize it, but I can't be sure."

Guppa took the rag, looked at it, sniffed it, and said at once, "Car wax." He looked at it again, squinted, twisted his lips into the musing expression of a movie detective during heavy ratiocination, and said to Marvin, "You—or someone else—used this rag to wax a green Studebaker Champion." He unfolded the rag slowly and held it up to the light, turning it this way and that, examining it minutely. With the rag as a shield, his face out of Marvin's sight, he winked at me. Oh, how that wink—his whole performance!—exhilarated me! I'd been wrong about him—he was going to be *terrific* on Flo and Freddie's show. "I'd say it was a two-door sedan," he said, nodding slowly. "Three—no—four years old." He handed the rag back to Marvin.

"Wow," said Marvin. "What an astonishing set of deductions."

"This is my friend Marvin," I said to Guppa, as if I'd never said it before. "He and I—"

"I'll bet you two are in the where-do-you-stop group together," said Guppa.

"Yeah," I said. Darn it. Guppa had gone too far. He forgot that he was supposed to have been making deductions from the evidence of the rag.

"That's right," said Marvin. He wore his mother's smile. "So," he said to me, "what do you notice about this rag that was used to wax a four-year-old green Studebaker Champion?"

"Notice?"

"Yup. What do you notice?"

"Well, it's dirty—"

"You're warm."

"It's got old wax on it—"

"Getting colder."

"And some of the paint—"

"Hot! Very hot!"

"The paint!" I said. "Of course!" Some of the paint had come off on the rag when Marvin's father waxed the car, just as it did whenever my father waxed our car. "Ah-*ha*!" I said. "It's part of the car! Part of the car is here on the rag."

"Right!" said Marvin. "The car has been extended! It doesn't stop where it used to."

"Say! You're on to something, boys," said Guppa.

"Guppa," I said. "Remember what you were telling me about trade-in value?"

"Huh?" he said, stretching his back again. For some reason, Guppa seemed to be having a harder and harder time following the thread of my conversations with him. At the time, without thinking much about it, I put this down to age—his, not mine. It didn't occur to me that perhaps my style was beginning to rival Miss Rheingold's in discontinuity.

"Trade-in value," I repeated.

"Trade-in value," said Guppa, so I'd know he'd heard.

"What is it again that makes the trade-in value go down? What do you call that?"

"Depreciation," said Guppa, with the pride all professionals take in the lingo of their guilds.

"It's like diffusion, isn't it?" I suggested. "Depreciation is like diffusion. Some of the value just drifts away." I remember quite clearly that at this point I got a little flustered. I may have stammered, and I'm sure I blushed. I fell victim to an unavoidable association. Diffusion put me in mind of Miss Rheingold's experiment

with her perfume, and that in turn brought Miss Rheingold herself
to mind, and with her came, of course, her legs.

"Well, I suppose in a way it is," said Guppa.

"But—um—I mean—I forgot what I wanted to say—" This was
a terribly embarrassing moment. Guppa stood there. Marvin stood
there. "Oh, I know—where does it go? I mean, where does the old
value go? You know, the old value of a car, when it depreciates."

"You mean, is there someplace where all the old value goes?"

"Sure there is!" said Marvin. "There would have to be, wouldn't
there?" He turned to Guppa for the wisdom of age.

"Well, I'm not exactly sure," said Guppa.

"What's left of the car, the part that isn't worth as much anymore, goes onto the used car lot," I said.

"Yeah," said Marvin. "But what about the rest of it? That must
go somewhere else."

"Some of it comes off on a rag when you wax it," I said.

"Sure," said Marvin, puzzling, "but there has to be more, a lot
more. The rest of it—the rest of it—" His eyes lit up. "—the rest
of it must just kind of slip into the *Zwischenraum*!"

"Yeah!" I said. "Into the *Zwischenraum*. The car winds up sort
of spread out all over the place."

"Wow!" said Marvin. "I never understood that before." He
turned his mother's smile on Guppa.

"*Zwischenraum*," said Guppa. "No kidding."

The three of us stood there in silence for a bit, but it was clear to
me that, despite this magnificent discovery, something unstated, a
question unasked, still hung in the air.

"Well," said Guppa, who must certainly have known that I had
something I wanted to say to him.

"Well," I said.

"Might as well get back to work," said Guppa.

"Might as well," I said.

"Where do we start?" asked Marvin. He stood there grinning.
After a while, the blank look on my face made him repeat himself:
"Where do we start?" He waited another moment, and then said,
"Get it?"

"Huh?"

"Where do we . . . *start*?"

"Oh. Sure," I said. "I get it. Sorry, Marvin. My mind was on something else. That happens to me. I—ah—I have a strange mind. You know, Marvin, I—I've been thinking about something. Do you ever watch 'Fantastic Contraptions'?"

"I used to," he said. "Before we started going to school all day."

"Well," I said, thinking that I might sneak up on the idea of collaboration, "I was thinking—"

Suddenly something like a verbal explosion occurred. I think that what I had to say had built to such a level within me that it couldn't be contained, there could be no more hemming, no more hawing, no more beating around the bush. It wanted out, and out it came, in a rushing burst: "Guppa, you should see what Marvin's mother makes—they're little trees with trunks twisted out of wire and wire branches that grow out from the trunks, and on the ends of the branches she hangs little bits and pieces of metal in lots of different shapes and some of them are even colored, and they whirl around in the slightest little bit of wind because they're so well balanced, and these little whirling bits of metal coruscate as they whirl—you know, catch the light—and they look just great even though they don't do anything, or I should say don't do anything more than catch the light, which turns out to be something pretty important, because I figured out that if you're going to win on 'Fantastic Contraptions' you have to have little bits of stuff like Mrs. Jones's windflowers—that's what she calls them, windflowers— just whirring and turning and catching the light, because people really like useless coruscations, although you'd have to say that they're not really useless because they do have a use—although I'm not sure whether their use is a less important or a more important use than the kind of use that we would usually think of as useful— but anyway it turns out, at least it seems to me, that little whirling bits like windflowers make the people in the audience laugh, and Flo and Freddie use them to make jokes about, which turns out to be pretty important, because when you get right down to it I think jokes are what Flo and Freddie's show is really all about, because they could have a show called 'Flo and Freddie's Amazing Chickens' and it wouldn't matter because the chickens would just be there as an excuse for Flo and Freddie to make jokes and tell stories about Flo's crazy uncles, so what I think would be a really good idea would be for you to get together with Mrs. Jones and have her make some really big windflowers to hold the trash can lids up instead of those posts that you have now, which are really just pieces of scrap wood, after all, and not even painted, and I think you'd have to admit that they don't look too good, but instead of those old posts you'd have really colorful tree trunks with windflowers on most of the branches except for one on each trunk that the trash can lid would hang from, but the people in the audience would hardly see it with all those bright flashing windflowers, even though it would still be doing its job, of course, and those windflowers might just be the key to success because something I'm starting to understand is that appearances count for a lot, as you've told me so often yourself about selling Studebakers, and as Porky says about the restaurant, 'It's got to have character, and if it's got character it doesn't really need anything else—in fact, the food doesn't even have to be any good,' so what do you say?"

While I was speaking, my whole body seemed to be working along with my mouth at the task of convincing Guppa that this was the thing to do. My hands gesticulated in a wild way, unrelated, as far as I could tell, to the substance of what I was saying, but eager to join in, and out of my control. Frequently they flew into my hair and tugged, flipped, and frazzled it, so that by the time I'd finished I resembled Quanto the Minimum after one of his dizzying flights.

Guppa was amazed. I think my presentation must have been so amazing that he couldn't have said anything but what he did, which was, "Well, okay, sure, why not?"

21

WHEN WE ARRIVED at the Joneses', Guppa wouldn't let Marvin just lead him into the house. He insisted on ringing the doorbell, and he stood there at the front door with his hat in his hand, as if he'd come courting.

When the door opened, he said, "Good afternoon, Mrs. Jones. I hope you remember me—I'm Herb Piper. I sold you your Champion. Down at Babbington Studebaker?"

"Why, of course, I remember you, Mr. Piper," said Mrs. Jones. "You're 'Call Me Herb.'"

"That's me," said Guppa. "And please do. Call me Herb. I think you know my grandson—Peter." Guppa sounded odd to me. This wasn't the way I ever heard him talk. It was his Studebaker voice.

"Yes, I do," she said. "Peter, *le roi*." She patted me on the head.

I expected Guppa to get right down to business now that the introductions were over, but instead he sniffed with extravagant gusto the aromas of Mrs. Jones's cooking that wafted out the open door. He rested a hand on my shoulder and said, "My, my, my, that smells good. May I ask you what that is you're cooking?"

"That? Oh, that's just a chicken. I'm making some chicken and dumplings."

"Chicken and dumplings!" said Guppa, as if he'd never heard of it before. "That sounds good. That sounds *very* good."

"We have that at home," I said, astonished. "Gumma makes that, too." Though I didn't recognize it, Guppa was selling. I was seeing his professional behavior. Apparently, flattery was part of his technique. If Mrs. Jones had said that she was toasting a slice of white bread, Guppa would have said that that sounded good, too.

What I would have found most surprising, if I'd seen it then, was the fact that Guppa was selling himself, he was working to sell himself, so that when he finally got around to suggesting collaboration, Mrs. Jones would be favorably disposed.

He tightened the hand on my shoulder and said, "My grandson Peter here has been telling me about your windflowers—but I'm surprised he didn't tell me about your cooking."

Now, I thought, now that he's brought the windflowers up, he'll get down to it, but he wasn't ready, not yet.

"How's that Champion running?" he asked.

"Why it's running just fine," said Mrs. Jones. "Mr. Piper, why don't you come in and have a cup of coffee?"

"That sounds nice," he said. "That sounds very nice. Come on along boys."

At least we were in the house. It couldn't take him much longer to get to the heart of the matter now, I thought—but it did. It seemed to take him forever, and he consumed more cups of coffee than I had ever seen him drink before, but finally he set his cup down and said, "I think I mentioned that Peter has been telling me about your windflowers."

"Yes, you did," said Mrs. Jones. "You did mention that."

"I wonder if I might see those?" Ah! At last!

"Of course, Mr. Piper. Come on out into the back yard, where Mr. Jones keeps his chickens."

Then it took no time at all. As soon as Guppa saw the windflowers, he saw their value. A smile formed on his face.

"Well, now, these are really something," he said.

"They aren't bad—" said Mrs. Jones.

"Very far from bad, Mrs. Jones," said Guppa. "They're really eye-catching."

"—but they're very small," she said. "Something big, now, something much bigger, as tall as a man, maybe even a little taller than that, well, that would be something."

Guppa turned toward me and winked, and then slowly turned toward Mrs. Jones and said, "Peter has an idea about how you and I might work together. It's an interesting idea—"

"The king has an interesting way of thinking," Mrs. Jones said.

"That's true," said Guppa. "Let me tell you about my garden—"

He did, and he described his automatic waterer, and then he described it as it might be, with the trash-can lids suspended from giant versions of Mrs. Jones's little windflowers. She was delighted. It turned out that what she'd said to Guppa about building giant windflowers was almost a confession. She considered the ones she'd made mere models for her future work. Almost from the first, she had wanted to make a leap in scale, but like so many people whose dreams seem to have no practical value she had kept them to herself. Guppa had brought with him a justification for dreaming—call it an excuse if you like.

"I have some supplies already," she said. "In the cellar. Some lengths of cable, scrap metal, paint. When would you like to start?"

"Right away, I suppose," said Guppa. "If that's okay with you. You see, Peter's really got his heart set on our getting on 'Fantastic Contraptions,' and he's sure we can do it with my waterer and your windflowers if we put them together so we've got—what are we going to call the things?"

There was only the briefest of hesitations. It was as if Mrs. Jones had had the whole project in mind for some time, as if she already knew about Guppa's invention.

"Waterwillows," she said.

22

FOR THE NEXT FEW DAYS, our back yard was a hive of industry. Marvin and Raskol hit it off right from the start—something that, I suppose, could have been predicted from the fact that both of them could look at a perfectly good drawing of a lighthouse and see a watch-tower—and the three of us launched into our work with an amazing burst of energy. It amazed me, and it sure amazed my father.

"You amaze me, Peter," said my father.

"Really?"

"Yes, you do, you really do. I wonder where all that energy has been hiding."

"Hiding?"

"Yes. How come I never saw a burst of energy like that when you were supposed to be helping us clear the hill from the back yard?"

"You mean before it was the hill, when it used to be a mound of debris?"

"Don't split hairs with me, Peter."

"I was younger then."

"That's true, Bert," said my mother.

"And I guess I was still getting over the measles."

"The measles?"

"I had the measles, didn't I?"

"You had the measles after we gave up on the hill."

"That's true, Peter," said my mother.

"Amazing how long the onset is," I said.

"Never mind," said my father.

"But isn't it astonishing that I should have been so weakened by the measles long before the symptoms even showed?"

"Forget it, Peter," said my father.

"Of course, I guess you could say that the weakness actually *was* the first symptom—"

"I said forget it," said my father.

I did. It was wise not to push these things too far.

WE WORKED ON THE TOWER each afternoon when the school day ended. All in all, the work took us a couple of weeks. The first week and nearly all of the second went into clearing bamboo from the site. Then we erected the watchtower in two days of frenzied work. (During those busy days I discovered what a pleasure it is to hear a hammer hit a nail squarely. I didn't hit the nail heads squarely very often, but when I did I was rewarded with the solid sound of competence. I found that I could hear that sound and get the satisfaction that came with it more often if I used a lighter touch, and I've applied that principle to all forms of work throughout my later life.)

I tapped away happily, occupying my mind with a chant to the rhythm of my tapping: *depreciation, bun soup, windflowers, court bouillon, Zwischenraum, shandy, ontology, epistemology, bills of lading, splines.*

When we were done, we gave the watchtower what I've thought of ever since as "the builder's look." If you watch someone completing almost any kind of work done with the hands, especially work that requires some skill or esthetic judgment or has been a real pain in the ass during the doing, you are likely to see the craftsman, at the end of the work, or merely at the end of one day's installment of it, pause to take the builder's look. It begins with stepping back and taking the long view. (For small work, holding-at-arm's-length serves as a stepping-back.) This stepping-back is essential, for you, the builder, *homo faber,* must be able to see your work in the round and in its surroundings. You want to see that the proportions are right, for one thing, and you want to assure yourself that what you've made really *is*, that it fills some space in this world that formerly was empty. If the proportions are right, and you've filled some space properly, you complete the builder's look with self-congratulation.

At the end of the first full day of real building, we had a pretty solid base, just a wooden platform, but solidly constructed. It had taken us all day, and when we had finished work that evening and were walking away from the site in the fading light, sweaty, tired, but exhilarated, we turned as if at a signal, and looked back at where we had been working, intending to take the builder's look. None of us said anything at first, but we were all immediately disappointed to find that our work didn't show. The foundation was well built, we knew that; we'd put our best effort, the best of the scrap lumber, and the straightest of our scavenged nails into it—but it didn't show. It was completely hidden by the bamboo. Work that doesn't show when you take the builder's look is disappointing. It could serve as one of the definitions of disappointment.

"Nice work, guys," said Raskol, but without much enthusiasm.

"I think you can see one corner of it from here," said Marvin.

"Really?" I said. I was trying.

"Maybe not from where you are," said Marvin, "but I think if you come over here—"

"Oh, yeah," I said, lying. "I think you're right."

"That might be it," said Marvin.

"I think that's just a leaf of bamboo," said Raskol.

"Hey, listen, we did a good day's work," I said. "A building's got to have a firm foundation."

"Sure," said Marvin.

"Oh, yeah, definitely," said Raskol.

"Tomorrow," I said, "we'll put up the uprights, and then you'll see that tower tower. You'll see it tower over the bamboo."

"Yeah," said Marvin.

"Sure," said Raskol.

"And we won't stop with the uprights, either, we'll add the platform at the top, the railing, the cabin where the guard can go to get in out of the rain, the housing for the searchlight—"

ENTHUSIASM is useful in a crew of builders, but there can be too much of a good thing. An excess of enthusiasm becomes impatience, and impatience is dangerous in any endeavor that must be done right, for work like that seems to have its own idea of how much time it deserves to take, and it can turn on you if you rush it. Looking back, I see a kind of frantic carelessness in our work the next afternoon. Annoyed by the time we'd had to spend clearing bamboo and the full workday we'd put into the foundation, we threw ourselves into the work with an impatient determination to finish by nightfall, and we did. From the first day's sturdy platform, four long uprights rose, tapering inward to support a smaller platform at the top. A railing ran around this platform, and in the center was a table, tall and gangling, that would hold the searchlight I'd made from the windup record player. The whole thing resembled my very first drawing, but it was even simpler and cruder, as if we had been working from a rough sketch I'd made *before* my first drawing. Neither Raskol nor Marvin seemed to notice or care how far short of the goal the realization had fallen, and I didn't want to hurt their feelings, so I said nothing about it.

As dusk came on, we finished. Walking across the yard, we turned to take the builder's look. Raskol, Marvin, and I stood there, congratulating ourselves, three pals who had accomplished something. We had built a watchtower. Considering it a little more disinterestedly, giving it a builder's look from thirty-five years' distance, I think that our impatience must have been responsible for the slight tilt I detected. I wondered what to do about it. Should I bring it up? Or should I let it go? Did I really see it? Or was it just the fading light playing tricks with my eyes? Was it, perhaps, the bamboo that was crooked? Maybe it had grown away from the prevailing wind, or toward the sun—something like that.

"Looks great," said Marvin.

"Yeah, great," said Raskol.

There was a silence. I tried tipping my head to one side. That made it look better.

"Does it seem to tilt a little?" I asked.

"Might just be the light," said Marvin.

"Or the bamboo," I said.

"The bamboo?" said Raskol.

"Leaning away from the wind?" I suggested.

"Or growing toward the sun?" suggested Marvin.

We stood in silence again. All of us tried tilting our heads a little. That really did make it look better. I seemed to need to tilt my head a little farther than before to improve it, though. Not only that, but I now seemed to see it begin to twist. The tower seemed to be turning itself so that it could show its top to us, as if it were bowing.

"Guess I better be getting home," said Marvin.

"Yeah, me too," said Raskol.

They seemed glum. "It looks great!" I claimed. I wanted to cheer them up. "Of course, it's pretty dark now, so we can't really see it too well. You know—dusk is a funny time of day. The light is weird—you know what I mean? It can play tricks on you. Sometimes things seem sort of—twisted."

They mounted their bikes and rode off, vanishing into the gathering dusk. I turned back for another builder's look. It was definitely tilting and twisting. I went inside for dinner.

AT THE TABLE, after we'd all filled our plates and begun to eat, I heard, from the direction of the watchtower, an eerie groan.

"What was that?" asked my mother.

"A dog howling," said my father.

"Probably," I said.

The groan subsided, rose again, subsided and rose again, and then twisted into a shriek like nails being drawn from wood.

"The poor thing," said my mother. "Do you think you ought to take a look, Bert?"

"Maybe," said my father.

"It's going to stop in a minute," I said.

The shrieking rose in pitch and volume.

"What makes you say that, Peter?" asked my mother.

"Just a hunch," I said.

There was one last, anguished shriek, and then a sigh. That must have been the platform and supports settling into the bamboo. Then there was silence.

"See?" I said. "I knew it would stop."

I kept my head down and ate.

23

GUPPA AND MRS. JONES were much more successful. She
worked in her basement, and Guppa sometimes worked there with
her, but they wouldn't let anyone see what they were doing, because they knew that it's best to keep the rough work out of sight
and show nothing until you're ready. Then, one day, as if they had
sprung up overnight, like mushrooms, beautiful otherworldly trees
sprouted throughout Guppa's garden, trees with twisted trunks of
many colors, smooth, arching branches, whirling multicolored
flowers, and dangling lemon-yellow trash-can lids—waterwillows.

THE WATERWILLOWS appeared in the garden on the day my father discovered that I'd cut the end from the garden hose. I was out
at the watchtower construction site, halfheartedly pulling nails from
salvageable boards when he arrived wearing a puzzled look. He
stood there for a moment with his hands in his back pockets, looking
around. He seemed not to be able to decide what was puzzling him.

"Peter," he asked, "do you know what happened to the nozzle of
the garden hose?"

"Huh?" I said.

"Someone cut the nozzle off the garden hose," he said by way of
clarification.

He was speaking to me, but he was still looking around, as if he
were looking for the cause of his puzzlement, as if something other
than the garden hose were puzzling him, possibly something he had
seen on his way out to the hill without really noticing it.

"Oh," I said.

He seemed to be about to speak again, but just at that moment, as he was looking around, the garden and, of course, the water-willows, caught his eye. He squinted at the sight, and for a moment he was frozen in that attitude. Then he shook himself and turned toward me again.

"Why did you cut the end off the garden hose?" he asked.

"You're assuming that I did it?" I said.

"Yes."

"Gee—"

"Why *did* you do it?"

He raised his head as if he were remembering something remarkable. Slowly he turned back toward the garden.

"I had to make sure that it would fit into the hole in the can without having a lot of air leaking around the edges," I explained, with, I think, admirable clarity.

"Uh-huh," he said. "I see." Then he said, "Can?" turning toward me again. "What can?"

"A potato-chip can."

"A potato-chip can?" He turned back toward the garden.

"Yeah. I got it at school," I said. "They were throwing it out at the cafeteria."

"Wait a minute," he said, his attention drawn back to me again. "*Why* did you have to fit the hose into this can?"

"Huh?" I said.

"Why did you have to fit the hose into a can?"

"You mean '*Why?*'"

"That's what I'm asking you."

"It was an experiment. For science. *General* science. You know, science education is pretty important for a person my age. It probably wouldn't be going too far to say that science is the most important subject. General science."

"Peter—" He had turned away from me again and was studying the garden.

"Oh, sure," I said. "I know a strong argument can be made for literature, and I bet you're about to make it, but a kid my age doesn't really have the experiences a person needs to really appreciate great literature, does he?"

"Peter—" he said again, still looking at the garden.

"Science, on the other hand," I went on, "really doesn't require much more than a receptive, flexible, reasonable mind—and I've got that. In fact, I'll probably never be more receptive to new ideas than I am right now. That's why it's so important for me to learn the experimental method."

"Never mind, Peter," he said.

"Knowing the experimental method can help me bring rigor to my thinking and keep me from falling into all kinds of logical error. Now you take shandy—"

"Never *mind*, Peter," he said. "Just tell me this—what the hell is your grandfather growing over there?"

"Oh," I said. "Those. It's kind of a long story."

24

THEN THE LODKOCHNIKOVS got a television set, and the center of my attention shifted at a stroke—not to the television set, but to Ariane's hip.

The Lodkochnikovs lived in a house on stilts at the very edge of the estuarial stretch of the Bolotomy River. They had gone without television longer than any other family I knew. My own parents had been holdouts, too. They had resisted long enough for me to begin to feel a little ashamed of showing up at neighbors' houses whenever a favorite program happened to be coming on, trying to seem ignorant of the schedule but always showing up just before the hour or the half hour. Since food, as the token of hospitality, must be offered even to the least of guests, I was served a lot of meals and snacks in those neighbors' houses, and politeness required that I eat them. I began to feel indebted and burdened by my debt. My friendships had begun to suffer from the feeling, so I was greatly relieved when my parents finally bought a set and I could stay at home, watch the programs I chose, and eat the snacks I favored. The Lodkochnikovs went without television for much, much longer. Year after year, despite the pleas of his wife and children, Mr. Lodkochnikov held out. He was just against it, he said. Then one day something snapped in him, and he came home with an antiquated set, a tiny screen in an enormous box. The family was dumbstruck. What, they wondered, could have brought about this change of heart? He never offered any explanation, and the others were wise enough not to press him for one. Some unknown, unexpected something had changed his mind—who cared what? Well, I did. It puzzled me.

He installed the set in a small, dark room at one end of the house, formerly used as a storeroom. Ariane and her mother cleaned it enthusiastically in anticipation of the arrival of the set, but the room still held the musty odor of a closed room, of neglect. That end of the house hung well out over the river, so at low tide the musty odor was augmented by the odor that permeated the entire Lodkochnikov house at low tide, the smell of Bolotomy River muck. They furnished the room with scavenged furniture: a couple of kitchen chairs, their seats and backs padded and covered with red plastic patterned to look like marble; two chairs with maple arms wide enough to invite you to rest your glass on them and curved enough to make it likely that the glass would slip, spill, and earn you a smack from Mr. Lodkochnikov; and, most important to my story, an enormous old sofa, each cushion sagging to a different level, originally upholstered in mud brown, but now covered with a couple of chenille bedspreads that Mrs. Lodkochnikov had sewn together and tucked and tacked and pinned to the frame. This slipcover I associated from the very first—guiltily, thrillingly—with bed and with Ariane and with Ariane in bed, because there was a chenille bedspread on my bed at home, and because if I dropped in at the Lodkochnikovs' before noon on a Saturday I sometimes caught a glimpse of Ariane wearing a white chenille robe. I made a practice of dropping in on Saturday mornings in the hope of catching such a glimpse. When I did, it pleased me to believe that under the white chenille robe she was wearing nothing.

I remember well that first night of television at the Lodkochnikovs'. Mr. Lodkochnikov sat proprietarily in the more upright of the maple chairs, smoking a cigar and drinking beer while he watched, commenting continually on what he saw, sometimes just murmuring an objection, sometimes anticipating the punch lines of the jokes, sometimes grumbling, sometimes just snorting. At some point in the evening I became aware that his attitude toward his television set had changed from pride to disappointment. I wish I'd been aware of the change earlier, when it began, so that I might have noticed and reported the process. It must have been gradual. If my senses, sensors, or sensibilities had been more refined, I could probably have detected it early on. There must have been signs—a certain twist of the mouth, the slightest lethargy in the way he knocked the ash from his cigar, measurably longer pulls at his beer bottle—but I didn't notice them. I saw the difference only when it became gross enough to be an obvious contrast to his earlier state, so it seemed to be something sudden and discontinuous, like one of Quanto's or Miss Rheingold's startling leaps.

Finally, he got up with a grunt and left the room. To tell the truth, the rest of us were glad to see him go. He'd become pretty vocal as his disappointment had grown, and by the time he left, his grumbling and snorting were even drowning out the commercials. We were happy to be alone and silent, sitting in the silver glow.

New television sets had been coming onto the market quickly for years, each new model offering advantages over the earlier ones—a larger screen, better sound, and so on, and people were quick to replace one set with a newer one. Mr. Lodkochnikov, through a network of contacts mysterious to me then but which I now think must have been based entirely on barroom encounters, had easy access to outmoded sets at the discounted prices of superseded technology. That very first evening, when he left the room in disappointment, he launched a hobby: he began a quest for the perfect television set. For a while there was a different set in the little room every time I visited. Now and then Mr. Lodkochnikov himself would come into the room and sit in the upright maple chair and watch his latest set for a while. His older sons, the two Ernies, would try to anticipate his comments about the shows and make them before he could, in voices low enough so that he wouldn't realize they were making fun of him. They didn't have to be particularly careful, though, because Mr. Lodkochnikov's fascination and annoyance with television ran so deep that he was oblivious to everything else while he watched. However, each time he gave television another chance, at some point, inevitably, the moment would come when he'd had enough; he would grunt, get up, and go off, disappointed again, and soon he would replace the set with a different one. Apparently what other people said about watching television had led him to expect more. He gave each set a fair trial, and when he didn't find what he expected, he went out and got another. He was trying to buy a set that didn't exist: one that got better programs.

For Raskol and me and the two Ernies and Mrs. Lodkochnikov and Ariane, this was not a problem. For us, there was lots worth watching, or, to be more accurate and honest, anything was worth watching. This was a time when the medium still fascinated people for itself. Just the idea of sitting in a room in your home and watching a little gray moving picture was a pleasure of its own, no matter what the show was, and certainly without regard to what its quality was. Whether the show was good or bad only partly determined whether the experience of watching it was good or bad. We weren't watching a show on television, we were watching television itself.

25

EVERY AFTERNOON, as soon as she got home from work, Ariane began watching television. Nearly every afternoon I watched with her. For hours and hours I watched movies and commercials on the Lodkochnikovs' television sets, but I can't recall one of them, even though I have a good memory for such things and can remember quite vividly certain movies and some favorite shows, personalities, actors, and actresses that I saw on television at home. The reason for this blind spot is that the cinematic memories that must be there are entirely obscured by another memory, one so bright that it obliterates all the others as the light of the sun obliterates the feeble light of distant stars. I can't recall the television programs because I'm blinded by the memory of Ariane.

She watched television with the kind of idle interest that was all the interest she brought to anything then. I now see how bored she was by life, at least by the life that was offered to her or seemed to be accessible to her then. She had finished high school and gone directly to work at Babbington Clam. She was marking time, waiting for her world to expand. Later, it did, but that's another story. At the time, she was penned, affectionately penned it's true, like a prize lamb, but penned all the same. Her boyfriends were scrutinized. Her enthusiasms were examined. Her time was monitored. Mr. Lodkochnikov was behind all this. His sons fled his control, spending as much time as possible out of the house, but Ariane may have had nowhere to go, or she may have decided that escaping into the TV room was safer and just as effective as leaving the house. Anyway, she watched a lot of television. The telephone and dates were the only things that kept her from it. Her phone conversations were strictly limited, and she wasn't allowed on dates during the week, so, from Monday through Friday she watched television all evening and all afternoon. When I became aware of this pattern I contrived to free my afternoons so that I could sit in the dank little room on the lumpy sofa, with the shades drawn, in the electric moonlight of the round-faced set, as close as I could get to Ariane.

At Babbington Clam, her day began at six. She finished at three, and, thanks to the Purlieu Street School, which had eliminated the need for split sessions, so did I. Each morning, my anticipation of the afternoon would begin, and it would distract me throughout the day. By rushing home from school, racing through my chores, leaving my school clothes in a heap, and riding so hard and fast that my legs burned, I could manage to show up at the Lodkochnikovs' back door, a little out breath, just as the afternoon movie was beginning.

Before I opened the door I executed a little ritual: I rested my hand on the door frame, put my forehead to the glass, and wished that Ariane would be alone. If the weather was good, the two Ernies were usually out somewhere getting into trouble; Raskol, who was disgusted with me for having given up on the tower, was usually out trying to make some money; Mrs. Lodkochnikov was out shopping or doing other chores; and my wish would be granted. When I opened the door, Ariane would just be settling down on the old sofa.

"I'm in here, Peter," she would call out, "in the TV room."

26

THE FIRST OF MY AFTERNOONS in that dark little room with Ariane came about by accident—or luck.

I had come by in all innocence, looking for Raskol. I knocked at the back door and waited. I heard someone calling, but I couldn't tell whether it was Ariane or Mrs. Lodkochnikov, and I couldn't tell what she was saying. I knocked again, louder. I heard someone calling again, still too faintly for me to understand. I put my hand against the door frame and leaned against the door, with my head against the window, and then I could make out who it was and what she was saying, faintly still, but clearly enough to understand. It was Ariane calling to me, "I'm in here, Peter, in the TV room."

I let myself in and walked through the house, with no particular expectations, no particular suspicion that she might be alone. I came into the little room, which was dark, as always, and found her curled up on one end of the sofa, like a cat, in the silvery light of the set.

She raised her finger to her lips to keep me silent, and I tiptoed across her field of vision and sat at the far end of the sofa, making an exaggerated business out of being quiet and not disturbing her viewing. When I settled into my place, I watched the movie for a moment or two, but my view of the screen was obstructed by an ironing board, and that got me thinking. Apparently, I reasoned, Ariane had been ironing or intended to start ironing. On the ironing board there was a piece of clothing. I looked it over and determined that it was a dress I had seen her wear often. A fascinating thought arose in my mind, unexpected and unwilled but quite welcome: the dress on the ironing board might be the dress Ariane had been wearing at work. When she got home she had made herself a snack and come into the TV room. She had set up the ironing board, intending to iron her dress, which had horizontal wrinkles across the front because she'd been sitting at the Babbington Clam switchboard all day. She had turned the TV on and found that she was just in time to catch the beginning of the afternoon movie. She had taken the dress off and tossed it onto the ironing board with the intention of ironing it while she watched the movie, but she had settled onto the sofa to eat her snack and gotten interested in the movie and hadn't bothered ironing the dress. It was a pleasant theory, because if it was correct it meant that Ariane was just a sofa's length away from me, alone in a darkened room, in her slip. To test the theory, all I would have had to do was take a peek, but I didn't want to, because I knew that if I did there was a strong likelihood that the assumptions and deductions from which the attractive theory was constructed would turn out to have been nothing more than wishful thinking and would collapse in a heap, like a doghouse suffering from cumulative error or a lighthouse built by kids.

Instead, I tried to verify the theory indirectly while I kept my eyes on the set. Memory wasn't much help. I'd seen Ariane when I came into the room, but she was curled up in a ball. True, now that I studied the memory of her curled there, she did seem to be wearing white. What I had assumed at the time to be a white dress might have been a slip. I sat at the end of the sofa, absorbing the sensations emanating from Ariane while pretending to pay attention to the television, the perfect mask for the attention I was paying to her. I was watching the images on the set, but all my other senses and all my thoughts were focused on her, only on her. I couldn't seem to hear the dialogue over the rustle of her stockings when she moved her legs, one stocking sliding against the other. I knew when to laugh only because she laughed. I sat beside her on that sofa for the entire afternoon, and she never got up to do her ironing. At last the phone rang. When Ariane jumped up from the sofa to take the call, I couldn't help looking at her, whatever embarrassment it might cause us both. She was wearing a white dress. Across the back, in red stitching, it was labeled Babbington Clam.

"Peter," she called from the hall. "It's your mother. You have to go home for dinner."

27

MISS RHEINGOLD SAT on the edge of her desk, holding the general science book open in front of her. Her habit of sitting on her desk and crossing and recrossing her legs had led most of the boys in the class—including me—to sit throughout general science in a rubbery slump with our eyes at the level of Miss Rheingold's desk top so that if she recrossed her legs carelessly we wouldn't miss the opportunity for some important extracurricular education. The long-term effects of this posture are likely to show up as nagging back pain in our golden years, but at the time the possibilities seemed worth any risk.

"All right," she said, "your assignment for last night was pages fifty-four through sixty-two in Chapter Three, 'How Frogs Jump,' and the sixty-four mimeographed sheets I gave you on the mathematical foundations of quantum theory. Do we need to go over that, or shall we move on?"

There was no response to this at all. We flipped the pages of our books, examined our pencils closely, and rustled our papers, trying to conceal our complete incomprehension. No one—certainly not I—dared even ask a question, the likelihood of asking something stupid was so great. Ah, but I was wrong. Matthew was willing to ask a question. He raised his hand.

"Matthew?" said Miss Rheingold.

"I'm a little uncertain about Heisenberg's uncertainty principle," he said, finishing with an urbane chuckle he had copied from a Cary Grant movie.

"Would anyone else like me to go over that?" asked Miss Rheingold. There was a great deal of throat-clearing, but no one was willing to admit—well, stupidity. "If not," she said, "then perhaps you'd be willing to come in this afternoon, Matthew, and I'll go over it with you then. It's quiet here when the building is empty. We'll be alone. We can really concentrate on your questions then." There was in her eyes an eagerness that we had come to recognize, something puzzling, thrilling, and unsettling.

"Miss Rheingold?"

"Bill?"

"Maybe it might be a good idea if I came in for some help with that, too. It's not that I don't get it, you know, but I'm having some trouble pronouncing the names—"

"Me, too," said Dave. "I could be free any afternoon this week."

"Same here," said Roscoe.

I had my hand up, but Miss Rheingold was already sliding off her desk and turning toward the green blackboard.

"Well," she said, "since it seems that quite a few of you have questions, why don't I go over it now."

She wrote "Werner Heisenberg" on the board.

"Ow!" said Matthew. Dave Botsch had hit his ear with a rubber band shot at short range.

"Let's imagine that we're back in 1926," said Miss Rheingold. "We've already got the quantum hypothesis, right?"

"Right," I said. It seemed safe to do so, and I didn't want her to think that I hadn't done the homework.

"Okay, so along comes a German scientist, Werner Heisenberg. Let's all say it: Vair-nair High-zen-bairg."

"Vair-nair High-zen-bairg," we said in unison, with the pleasant conviction that we were making progress.

"Good. Now here's the problem Heisenberg noticed. Let's say we have a particle. We want to be able to make some predictions about it. We want to know where it's going to be and how fast it's going to be moving some time in the future."

"Miss Rheingold?"

"Yes, Matthew?"

"That's one of my problems. Why do we want to know where it's going to be and how fast it's going to be moving in the future?"

"Why?"

"Why."

"Well, we—I—" She seemed not to know. Our embarrassment for her was immediate, and we were annoyed with Matthew for having rattled her.

"That's okay," said Matthew, just as concerned for her as any of the rest of us. "It's not important. Go ahead."

"No. It is important," said Miss Rheingold.

"You might want to shoot it," said Bill.

"What?" said Miss Rheingold.

"Like a duck," said Bill. "Or a frog, for that matter. You've got to know where to aim and how much to lead."

"Oh. Well, yes," said Miss Rheingold. "It could be something like that."

"Or you might want to avoid it," Bill went on.

"Yes?" said Miss Rheingold.

"Like a car coming at you," he offered.

"Right," said Matthew. "I get it."

"Or maybe," said Bill, emboldened by success, "you want to know just because the future of this one particle is crucial to the whole foundation of your understanding of the world. I mean, if you can't predict what this particle is going to do, then all your assumptions about what's going to happen next come crashing down like a house of cards. If you can't make predictions based on what you know now, then you can't tell *what* might happen to you."

"It's true," Miss Rheingold said, her voice breathy and hushed.

"Ever since I read those sheets you gave us on Heisenberg," Bill confessed, wringing his hands, "I feel that the future is a—a—"

"A muddle," offered Miss Rheingold.

"Right," said Bill. "A scary muddle. And it's got me kind of—well--upset—disturbed—"

"Uncertain," said Miss Rheingold.

She brought the fingers of her right hand to her mouth and tugged at her lower lip, squeezing it gently.

"Yes, that's it," said Bill. "Uncertain. Completely uncertain. You know what I mean?"

"Yes, I do," said Miss Rheingold. Her eyes shone and the smile on her lips was very queer. "I remember when I was in college and came upon the uncertainty principle for the first time." She had the distant look of a person looking into the past. "I felt that nothing I did really mattered. I felt—cut loose. I had a sudden, powerful desire to indulge in the most irresponsible behavior. I wanted to—"

"Maybe we could talk about this after school," suggested Bill.

"Yes," said Miss Rheingold. She shuddered slightly. "Yes. Maybe that would be a good idea. Why don't you come by at the end of the day?"

"I'll do that," said Bill.

Miss Rheingold turned back toward the board to make a dot that would represent a particle. Bill bestowed a small, brief, triumphant smile on the class, gathered his mimeographed sheets into a pile and rubbed his face in them.

"So," said Miss Rheingold, indicating the dot. "Let's say we have a particle whizzing by—"

"Like a duck," said Nicky.

"If it helps you to think of it that way, that's fine. In order to predict where this particle will be and how fast it will be moving, we have to know where it is and how fast it's moving now. How do you suppose we would find that out?"

"We'd measure it," I said, in the hope that Miss Rheingold wouldn't forget me.

"Right," she said. "And to do that, we have to find it. How do we usually find something?"

"We look for it," said Matthew, competing, as we all were.

"Good," said Miss Rheingold. "And if it's too dark to see it?"

"Shine a light on it," I said.

"Very good, Peter," she said. "That's what we could do. We could shine a light on the particle. Some of the light will be reflected. Now, if it's something big, like a duck, quite a lot of light will be reflected. Enough for our eyes to detect. Then we can see the duck."

"And shoot it," said Nicky.

"Yes," said Miss Rheingold, "if that's what we want to do. But you're getting ahead of me—"

"Blam!" said Nicky.

"Let's forget the duck for a moment, Nicky," said Miss Rheingold, "and go back to the particle."

"Hey, Barber," called Nicky. "Fetch, boy! Get that duck."

"Nicky!"

"Sorry, Miss Rheingold," said Nicky. "It's the call of the wild."

"Well you'll have to ignore it while you're in class," she said. "We are considering a particle, remember, not a duck. We want to be able to see the particle—or have some kind of detector see the particle—so that we can learn its speed and direction. So we decide to shine some light at it. We don't want to use a lot of light. We don't want to blast the poor little particle with a shotgun, do we, Nicky?"

"I guess not," Nicky admitted, reluctantly.

"So let's use as little light as we can," said Miss Rheingold. "Biff, you're in the where-does-the-light-go-when-the-light-goes-out group. What is the smallest bit of light we can use?"

"The smallest?" said Biff.

"One photon," said Matthew.

"That's right, Matthew," said Miss Rheingold, "but you should have given Biff a chance to answer."

"Yeah," said Nicky. "Six or seven years, he might have gotten it."

"Biff, can you give us an idea of what a photon is?" said Miss Rheingold.

"It's, um—"

"Biffy, she didn't ask you to do it," said Nicky. "She just asked you if you *could* do it. You can answer that one, can't you?"

"No," said Biff.

"Good going," said Nicky.

"All right," said Miss Rheingold. "Who knows? Matthew?"

"It's a single quantum of electromagnetic radiation."

"Good," said Miss Rheingold. "Now—"

"Wait a minute," said Nicky. "Wait a minute. That's what's wrong with science, right there. It's the only subject where the more you learn the less you know. A minute ago, we were talking about a photon. Okay, that's fine, a photon. I can at least say it. It was a little bit of light. I got that. If the bell had rung then, I would've been okay. I could've gone home, and when my father asked me what I learned in school today, I could've told him that a photon is a little bit of light. But now it's something else—I couldn't even tell you what. And now I *don't* get it. I went from *getting it* to *not getting it* instead of the other way around, you see what I mean?"

"Let's see if we can make it clearer," said Miss Rheingold.

"I think I can make an analogy, Miss Rheingold," said Matthew, so eager to please her that he was willing to risk another rubber band at close range.

"Here we go," said Nicky.

"If a beam of light from a flashlight is like a shotgun blast," said Matthew, "then one photon is like one BB."

"Okay," said Miss Rheingold, "but we should be aware of the differences. For one thing, there are many, many more photons in a beam of light than there are BBs in a shotgun shell."

"Is it more like one sperm in a handful?" asked Bill.

"There's a danger in analogies—" said Miss Rheingold.

"*Now* I get it," said Nicky. There was a rumble of suppressed laughter from the back of the room. "Hey, shut up," said Nicky. "It's an analogy."

"In any case," said Miss Rheingold, "even if we use only *one* photon, the point is this: the photon will disturb the particle. It will change its speed and direction."

She looked around the room to see if we had understood, and everywhere she saw smiling faces mirroring her own, but she didn't see that we were smiling to hide our fear that this was going to get even more complicated.

"But, it gets even more complicated than that!" she announced with a glee that is difficult for me to describe. What she felt was not a simple pleasure. She loved complexity. She was the first person I had ever met who did. "If we're trying to get a good idea of where the particle is," she continued, "we want to use light with a short wavelength. You people in the where-does-the-light-go group probably know why, but I'll explain for the others."

She paused for a moment, gathering her thoughts. Then she drew a rippling wave along the board and launched into an explanation of the wave nature of light, the measurement of wavelength, and so on, concluding with, "so, as the wavelength gets shorter, the photon's energy becomes greater, and as the wavelength gets longer, the energy of a photon becomes less. The greater the energy of the photon we're shooting at the particle, the more it's going to disturb the particle. But the shorter the wavelength, the better we know where the particle is. So, you see, the more we know about where it is, the less we know about how fast it's moving. The more we know about how fast it's moving, the less certain we are about where it is. Uncertainty! Isn't it thrilling?"

I know I wasn't alone in feeling the uneasiness I felt. I'm certain all the others felt as I did. I had assumed, without ever examining or expressing the assumption, that my young life rested on a base of certainty, and my notion of science—unconsidered, unexpressed though it was—had included an expectation like Nicky's, the idea that science would bring me more and more certainty, that the closer I looked the more I would know, the more I knew the more I would understand, and the more I understood the more clearly a single, simple, immutable plan would be revealed to me. Miss Rheingold had disappointed these unexamined expectations, and she went right on doing so.

"Now here's what Heisenberg figured out," said Miss Rheingold, nearly breathless with pleasure. "We can never get rid of this uncertainty." Her eyes had that uncanny brightness again. "It doesn't matter what we do. It doesn't matter what kind of particle we use or how we try to measure its properties." She supported herself against her desk as if she might fall. That queer smile played across her lips. "We can never know exactly where the particle is or exactly how fast it's going." She drew a deep breath. "Never. There will always be some uncertainty. That's life." She fell silent. She had begun to play with her lower lip again.

"Any questions now, Barber?" Nicky whispered.

28

ARIANE WAS IN THE KITCHEN when I arrived for my next afternoon of television with her.

"Butter that toast!" she said as soon as I came through the door.

It had just popped up. The butter was cold, straight from the refrigerator, and I had a tough time getting it to spread on the toast. I tried to cut the thinnest slices of butter I could, but the knife kept slipping and clanking against the butter dish. Ariane was at the stove, frying some slices of baloney for sandwiches. A glorious inner warmth spread through me when I realized that she had been expecting me: there were four slices of toast; there were two plates; one of the sandwiches was going to be mine.

"Fry! Fry!" she implored the baloney. To me she said, "We've got about a minute and a half before the movie starts. Think we can call these done?"

The slices had curled so that they looked like halves of a pink Spalding rubber ball. I considered this quite an early stage in the process of frying baloney. I liked my fried baloney dark. In fact, I liked to turn the hemispheres over at the end and let their rims turn black and crunchy, but I could see that Ariane was in a hurry. "Done," I said.

With a spatula, she lifted the baloney from the pan and started throwing the sandwiches together.

We heard the theme of the afternoon movie. "Oooo," she said. "Get in there, Peter, so you can tell me what happens."

I went to the television room to wait for her. "They just put a commercial on," I called out to reassure her.

The ironing board was up again, but there was nothing on it.

Ariane came dashing into the room. She handed me a plate with one of the fried baloney sandwiches on it. Then, as an afterthought, she handed me the other one, too.

"Hold this a minute, will you?" she asked.

I took it and sat there with my hands full while she reached around behind her, unhooked and unzipped her dress, let it drop to the floor, stepped out of it, and draped it over the ironing board. There she was, just as I'd hoped, in her slip.

"I don't want to make a mess of that," she said, "now that I have to wear my own clothes to work." She took her plate, curled up at her end of the sofa, and took a bite of her sandwich.

"No more Babbington Clam across the back?" I asked, amazed that my mouth worked, that my voice sounded quite normal.

"Nope. I got promoted. I'm the receptionist now. I have to look gorgeous."

I wanted to say, "And you do," but I didn't have the nerve. At her end of the sofa, she had contrived to curl herself up in the space of a single cushion. She rested her left arm on the arm of the sofa, and she balanced her sandwich plate there, too. She had her legs curled under her, her knees away from me, so that she presented to me a landscape round and soft that suggested comfort as much as sex: the shimmering nylon bulges of her buttocks, the line of her thigh, curving away like a country road, the lenticular pink undersides of her toes.

"Wonderful," I said. "Great, just great." I was congratulating her—and myself. I understood the kind of thrill Heisenberg must have felt when he discovered uncertainty. I'd made a discovery of my own: apparently, wishing could make things so.

"Thanks," said Ariane.

"It's terrific," I said. "Terrific." The thought had come to me that if she now had to be so careful about her clothes, I was facing the delightful prospect of finding her in her slip every afternoon when I arrived to watch the movie with her.

"Shhh," she said.

My future seemed seamlessly delightful, every day an afternoon, every afternoon a movie, with every movie Ariane. Amazing. I shifted slightly, ever so slightly, not enough, I hoped, to betray my true interests in the little room, but enough so that I could see Ariane much better, enjoy her, study her. She seemed to glow with lunar beauty—thanks to the silver light of the television set. I took a long, deep breath and was delighted to find in it, along with the rich odor of the Bolotomy flats beneath us, the mildewed sofa cushions, the hot iron, the toast and butter, the baloney, something sweeter, the scent of perfume, Ariane's perfume. "It's wonderful," I said. "It's great. It's—"

"Peter," she said. "Shut up. Watch the movie."

"Sure," I said. "Sure.

I rested my arm along the back of the sofa, and I passed the rest of the afternoon, while something or other happened on the screen, blissfully watching each tiny movement she made, inhaling her perfume, and slowly, slowly, slowly advancing my fingers closer to her.

29

ONE AFTERNOON, when I got home from school, I found a stack of cartons just inside the front door. Each of them was addressed to me. I rarely got mail of any kind—I was still a child, after all—and packages were rarer still, so the arrival of these packages would have been an unexpected treat if I hadn't been expecting it, which I had been ever since the night when, sitting at the top of the stairs out of my parents' sight, listening to the television show they were watching, I had heard them discussing the idea of buying me the encyclopedia I'd been lobbying for and, to my astonishment, deciding in favor of it.

"I know it would help him," said my mother. "He can find everything he needs to know there. I read that—"

"It's okay," said my father. "You don't have to try to convince me anymore. I've been convinced."

"You're sure?"

"I'm sure. I was sure a while ago."

"You were?"

"Yup."

"Why didn't you say so?"

"Well, at the time I didn't know I was convinced."

"Are you teasing me?"

"No."

"When *did* you know?"

"Ella, the show's back on."

"Just tell me when you knew. Was it when I said that the Munsons were getting one for Lorraine?"

"Um, no, I think it was after that."

"You're sure? You got kind of a funny look then."

"It might have been something on the TV."

Carefully, I crept back into my room and got into bed. I never did learn what argument had convinced my father. My past is full of holes like that. In fact, it would be more accurate to say that most of it is nothing, *Zwischenraum*, vast vacancies that separate tiny particles of knowledge.

My eavesdropping had robbed me of the pleasure of surprise, but compensated me with the pleasure of anticipation. If I hadn't known in advance that these packages were coming, I wouldn't have experienced the anticipation, sweet pain that we love and hate. Of course, I had to fake surprise to give my mother her part of the pleasure to be gotten from the encyclopedia, and I did.

"What are these?" I asked. "Are these for me?"

"They're addressed to you," said my mother.

"What are they?"

"Guess," she said, hugging herself.

I hefted them, shook them, held them to my ear, sniffed them, and guessed—candy, handkerchiefs, records—while my mother giggled and shook her head, until at last she couldn't stand it any longer and said, "Go ahead, open one."

"If I open one, will I know what's in the others?" I asked.

She thought about this for a moment, and from the look on her face—the little smile, the light in her eyes—I knew that I'd asked just the right question. (That's the one that surprises us, makes us think about a thing in a way we hadn't even thought of thinking of it before, the one that makes the thing a little more intriguing.) "Well," she said, "you will and you won't."

"I will and I won't." I faked a frown.

"That's right," she said. "In a way, you'll know what's in all the other boxes once you open any one of them. But in another way, you'll probably *never* know everything that's in them. You'll probably never even know all of what's in any *one* of them."

I put on a look of puzzlement. "What does that mean?" I said.

"Open one and find out," she said.

Opening the packages turned out to be a pleasure all its own, one I've never forgotten. Every package I've opened since has had a sweet association with the packages that held those books. Each volume was individually wrapped within a carton of its own. My mother and I unpacked the books and lined them up on the floor. We had no bookcase for them. The cardboard and wrapping accumulated in a heap, a messy jumble, like my state of mind following the research I had been trying to do, something to be discarded. The alphabetical, rectilinear orderliness of the books said that knowledge was orderly and limited. They seemed to promise a short, direct path to a neat, clean answer to my Big Question. The truth was, though, that I already knew there was no short path, because I had tried using encyclopedias at school. Instead of finding the answer to the question in them, I had found a fascinating place to wander. *That* was why I wanted a set at home. In the years that followed I sometimes used my encyclopedia in the usual way, as a reference—I "looked things up"—but only when I had to, because I really didn't think that was the best use for the books. They were much better thought of as a town, where I was a tourist, invited to ramble through the streets, with no obligations or destinations to keep me from rambling. Invited to ramble that way, to explore the side streets, peek into the houses, who would choose to walk a straight line along the high street? Not me, certainly not at eleven, and not yet at forty-six. Time enough later for the grim business of getting somewhere.

I read through the encyclopedia, book by book, but not from beginning to end, not deliberately and not thoroughly. I wandered it like a child crawling through tall weeds, rambling, like a walker without a compass or a map, who chooses his route from the sound of the street names, going nowhere, anywhere, everywhere, for the pleasure of the going, of meandering, a pleasure different from any I'd gotten from books before.

Every book promises something. You know that feeling just before you begin reading: the delightful anticipation of that something, the thing that this book will yield to you. Of course, some books never deliver the promise of that anticipatory moment, but even the worst of books has something in it. The magnificent thing about the books I was unwrapping was that they promised not just something but everything, and at that moment when the encyclopedia arrived I realized that everything was exactly what I wanted to know. Years later, when I began to write books myself, I knew—and this is the first time I've said it—that I really wanted to write a book about everything.

I opened one of the books and began reading. I wish I could remember where I began. What article was it? With my mother looking over my shoulder, I would probably have chosen something related to Miss Rheingold's question, but what? We'd been taught to use "key words" in a question to decide what topic to consult in an encyclopedia, but there were no entries for *where*, *do*, *you*, or *stop*. Maybe I didn't choose an article related to the question. Maybe I just opened a book at random. It doesn't matter now; that is, it doesn't matter for this reminiscence, but it matters a great deal for the progress of my intellectual development at eleven, because the first article led me to all the rest. I began reading, and I read until dinnertime, following the cross-references that led from that one article to another, from that to another, and from another to another, following the route of cross-references, a stroll defined by divagation, a diversion at every corner.

I was annoyed by articles without cross-references. I doubted that one little article could be all there was to say on a subject. Could this really be the last word? Was there nothing else related to this topic? At first, I tried getting out of these dead ends by backing up. I'd retreat an article or two along the irregular path I'd been following until I came to a cross-reference I hadn't chosen. Then I'd take that route instead of the one I'd followed originally and hope that it would put me on a longer trail, but I didn't care for that technique. Progress is satisfying; regress is not. Backing up felt like acknowledging a mistake. It made my having come to a dead end feel like something to be ashamed of, as if I should have known that a particular reference would lead nowhere, was a route not to be taken, as if I ought to have been able to anticipate my moves dozens ahead, like a chess master, and choose only the routes that went somewhere. I told myself that it was foolish to think that way, because if some paths weren't really meant to be taken, that would mean that some of the entries weren't really meant to be read; they were just taking up space in the books, a joke of the compilers.

(It never occurred to me at the time that this might in fact be the case, but years later, when I worked for the venerable firm that published *The Young People's Cyclopedia,* I relieved the tedium of long days in a windowless office by concocting entries for people and places that had never existed and mapping referential mazes that would send young researchers spinning into bottomless vortices of misdirection. These were articles that no one would ever "look up," since they had no referents in fact, nothing in them that anyone would ever need to know, but they would, I hoped, amuse the curious wanderer, the kind of encyclopedia-reader I had been.)

Sometimes I got out of cross-referential dead ends by simply jumping to the next article, or to another on the same page, or flipping the pages until something else caught my eye, but this felt wrong, like leaping a fence into some stranger's yard and dashing through to the next street, or leaping like Ping-Pong balls from mousetrap to mousetrap across a tabletop. It was a short, easy way out of the cul-de-sac, but taking the easy way out was ignoble. The noble thing to do, it seemed to me, was to swallow your pride, retrace your steps, and find out how things were connected, and when there were no paths provided, cut your own, so that you could, and eventually would, get everywhere, know everything.

My mother called me to dinner just as I decided all that. At the table, my father, rightly proud of himself for having bought the encyclopedia for me, said, "Tell me what you've learned so far." The poor guy probably wanted a fact or two, just something to show him that I'd opened the books and could remember something from them, but I was full of my idea, and blathered on and on about it. I tried to give him the whole thing, lead him along the whole path I'd followed, and bring him to the conclusion I'd reached.

"That's enough, Peter," he said when he'd had enough. "Eat your dinner."

"All knowledge is interrelated," I said, wrapping it up in a hurry.

He was stunned. My mother was stunned. I was stunned. Where did I get that idea? Did I mean it? Did I believe it? Was it true? Was I on to something? Or was I just a kid showing off? I stirred my peas into my potatoes silently, wary of saying another word.

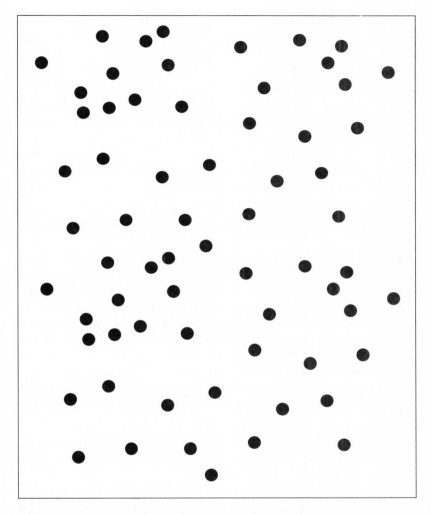

Figure 6: Multipurpose diagram showing black dots separated by white regions illustrates (a) separation of peas by regions of mashed potatoes, (b) separation of marble chips by concrete in a terrazzo mix, (c) separation of outstanding moments by the gray mush of memory, (d) separation of little bits of matter by regions of nothing (Zwischenraum). *Note that a photon directed at this diagram is more likely to hit nothing (or mashed potatoes, or concrete, or gray mush) than bits of matter (or peas, or marble chips, or outstanding moments).*

30

"ISN'T IT INTERESTING the way all knowledge is interrelated?"
I said.

"Not now, Peter," said Ariane. "Wait for the commercial."

I knew I was breaking Ariane's rule by speaking to her during a
movie, but I was out to impress her, and I was impatient. I had
brought a volume of my encyclopedia with me that afternoon, Volume C (Cat paradox; Causality; Cavendish laboratory; Combination lock; Como conference; Complementarity; Compound nucleus, theory of; Copenhagen school of physics; Correspondence principle), hoping that she would appreciate the intellectual patina I
was acquiring, but I'd arrived a little late, the movie had already
begun, and she didn't want to be diverted. I couldn't calm down.
Why wouldn't the damn movie hurry up? Why did she have to pay
such close attention to it anyway? I began to fidget. I opened the
book. I turned some pages. I closed the book. I stretched. I
opened the book again. I closed the book again. I shifted position.
I crossed my legs. I uncrossed my legs. I recrossed my legs. Finally she said, "*Will* you settle *down*?"

"Sorry," I said. I tried to sit still. I opened the book again. I
tried to read. I tried to breathe slowly and regularly. As I worked
to control my breathing, I became aware, again, of the odors in the
room—the mustiness of the sofa on which we sat, the slightly
scorched fabric of the dress Ariane had been ironing, the cabbage
soup drifting in from the kitchen, the river below us, and the aroma
of Ariane. Little by little, her delicious scent seemed to displace all
the others. *It's diffusion,* I thought. *Like Miss Rheingold's perfume.* This thought was, of course, accompanied by a vivid mental

image of Miss Rheingold's legs, but it faded quickly, overwhelmed by a dazzling thought. *Ariane's diffusing. She's filling the room.* I took a long, deep breath. *I'm inhaling Ariane.* I took another breath, deeper, and another and another. I tried swallowing as I breathed, swallowing the aroma of her.

"*Now* what?" she said. "Are you snoring?"

"Sorry," I said. I—"

"Come here," she said. Magically, she patted her hip. Oh, that hip, that hip, that satiny, slip-covered hip. That smooth expanse, where the satin stretched over the rounded prominence of it! That hip! The silvery sheen of the television light (released when electrons struck the fluorescent coating inside the television tube—Volume T) formed a vaguely ellipsoid brightness around it, like the contour line around a drumlin (Volume D) on a geological survey map (Volume M). Oh, that hip! I did as she suggested, acting quickly, so that she wouldn't have time to reconsider, but with great care not to appear too eager. I pivoted on the sofa. I stretched myself out. I began to lower my head toward that glowing hip.

I wasn't quick enough. She pulled a pillow from the back of the sofa and padded herself with it before head hit hip. I hid my disappointment and settled onto the pillow. She put her hand on my chest and patted me as if I needed comforting.

"There," she said. "Now just settle down. Settle down and shut up until the commercial."

Did she know how I felt, reclining there against her, how she made me feel? At the time I supposed that she didn't. I thought I was getting away with something. Now I think otherwise. I think she understood me better than I did myself. I think she was being generous to me, but I think she got something out of having me leaning against her, too. She couldn't have failed to see how fascinated I was by her, and my fascination must have been flattering. She must have liked knowing that she was responsible for the pounding of my little heart, and she couldn't have failed to feel it pounding beneath her hand.

The scent of her at close range, so dense, so rich and delicious, quite befuddled me. Inhaling, I was reminded of the time, years earlier, when I had gone with a school group on a tour of a candy factory. At the end of the tour we were invited to take a piece of chocolate from a barrel of imperfect pieces, misshapen rejects that had been culled from the line by sharp-eyed ladies wearing hair nets. I took one, but I didn't eat it until the next day because breathing in all that chocolate aroma had filled me up. Ariane's aroma was richer than that, much richer.

"Hey, Peter. Peter."

"Hm?" She was shaking me, and with each shake I was pressed for an instant closer to her, the skimpy pillow compressed between my head and her hip.

"It's the commercial," she said. "What were you going to tell me?"

"Oh. Um—" I didn't remember, but that didn't matter. I had other things to say to her. "Did you ever think about the way we smell things?"

"No," she said, shaking me again. "I didn't. What about it?"

"Well, when we smell things, there are molecules of the thing, whatever it is we're smelling, like cabbage soup or perfume or whatever, in the air."

"Mm."

"And when we smell them, we take them in, we breathe them in. Molecules of the thing. Whatever it is, the thing we're smelling."

"No kidding."

"Yes. I mean no. And just now I've been—"

"Uh-oh. Shhh. It's coming back on."

"But—"

"Next commercial."

I slumped back down against her again. I wiggled a bit, twisted my head against the pillow to shift the stuffing aside and thin it out, to get closer to her hip, and she tightened her grip on me to make me stop squirming. I lay there, inhaling her and waiting for the commercial. I had no patience for the movie that day. I lived for the commercials. I loved the commercials. I loved the instant when I realized that one was coming, the interval between the cessation of the image of the movie and the commencement of the image of the commercial, because in that moment when the screen was empty, Ariane stretched, yawned, rolled, shifted in a dozen delightful ways that I, resting as I was against her, felt reverberate through me like deep waves along a fault line (Volume E). That instant of recognition was the thin boundary between the anticipation of pleasure and the onset of pleasure. During the movie, Ariane wanted to watch, and she would tolerate no interruption, but the commercials bored her, so she was willing to listen to me then; she'd allow me to put on my little show, display my nickel's worth of learning. In the commercial breaks, I was the entertainment.

"So?" she said. "About the way we smell things?"

"Oh." The commercial had taken me by surprise. "Well, these molecules— You know what? It's not just about that. It's about the commercial, too."

"What? This commercial? This stuff for dainty feminine hand-washables?"

"Not just this one. All of them. There's a second where the show stops but the commercial hasn't started yet. Less than a second. It's a time when there's just nothing, well not nothing but just the snow—"

"What on earth does this have to do with how we smell things?"

"It's all tied up together. See, when something has a smell, it's got a cloud of molecules of itself spreading out from it, so you could say that it's not just where it was anymore. It's all over. Well, not all over, but it's much larger."

"You mean the cabbage soup is filling the house."

"Yes, yes."

"It's not just in the pot anymore, it's kind of all over."

"That's it."

"Disgusting."

"But wait," I said. "It's us, too. And used cars. Depreciation. And diffusion. It's about where we stop." I sat up suddenly. "It is!" I said. I had surprised myself. I'd discovered something about the question. "It is! You think you stop here, at your skin—"

I touched her. Without thinking about the liberty I was taking, I put my hand on her leg. Of course, I wasn't actually touching Ariane; I was touching her stocking. Still, I was much closer to touching her than I had been with the pillow between us. Apparently I was too close, because she slapped my hand and said, "Down, boy."

"Sorry," I said, though I was not sorry at all. "But the thing is that you don't stop here." I hesitated a moment, then touched her finger, just barely touched it, to show her what I meant. "This isn't the edge of you. It looks like it, but it isn't. Little bits of you are spreading out. All over the room. I know they are, because I can smell them."

"That's sick."

"No, no. It's not," I said. "You smell great. I love smelling you."

"Peter!" she said with a grimace. "If you don't cut this out, you're going to have to go home."

"No—wait—listen," I said. "When I smell you, I—well—you and I—"

"What are you getting at?" She looked suspicious.

"Some of you is in me," I said breathlessly.

"What!"

"It must be," I said with a shrug. "Maybe it goes back out when I breathe out, but for a while some of you is in me. We're all mixed up. I know it doesn't look that way, but it's true. It must be."

"You've got a strange mind, Peter," she said.

"Thanks," I said. "I wonder—"

"That's enough," she said, nodding at the screen, where the movie was back on. "Next commercial."

"Oh," I said. "Okay." I had been about to raise the interesting question of where our boundaries would lie if I licked her. It was probably best that I didn't. She would probably have sent me home. I settled down. She pressed that firm, steadying hand on me again. During the commercial break, while I was speaking so excitedly, the pillow had fallen to the floor. Throughout the next stretch of movie neither of us said a word. Neither of us seemed to notice that the pillow was gone. At least one of us was pretending.

WHEN I GOT HOME that evening, my mother gave me an odd look and sniffed and wrinkled her nose. "Whew!" she said. "Where have you been this time?"

"What do you mean?" I asked. Did she know? How did she know? Was it written all over my face?

"You smell funny," she said. "Like cabbage—and—" She sniffed some more.

"Oh," I said, backing away before she could guess the other scent. "I was at Raskol's. They're cooking cabbage soup."

"I think you brought it all home with you," my mother said. I was already on my way out of the room. "Go change your clothes and wash up. Put your sweater in the bag for the cleaners."

I went up to my room and got changed, but before I went back downstairs I held my sweater to my face and took a long draft of cabbage soup and Ariane.

31

I WORKED HARD that night and all the following weekend. I drew diagrams, changed them, redrew them, made more changes, and redrew them again. I wrote, changed what I wrote, rewrote, made more changes, and wrote again. I didn't seem to get anywhere. In fact, by Sunday night I seemed to be worse off than when I started. The idea that seemed so bright when it was leaping and darting and fluttering through my mind looked dull and dead when I'd caught it and pinned it to my paper. In writing it out, I had changed it. In my mind, still an idea, it had been ragged and confused, but interesting. When I wrote it out, I tried to impose on it the kind of orderly reasoning I found in my encyclopedia. The idea as I wrote it on paper made more sense, but it *only* made sense. It wasn't an idea now, but the representation of an idea. It didn't fly, didn't flutter by, didn't catch the eye as I thought it would. Something was missing, something vital, but I couldn't provide or restore it because I didn't know what it was.

The next Monday, the school-age population of Babbington again reached a critical mass. Three new kids were standing awkwardly at the front of my homeroom, but every seat in the room was filled, every seat in the school was filled. There was an atmosphere of crisis: we were marched to the auditorium, where the superintendent of schools, Mr. Simone, announced that we were going to have to go on split session again. At the end of the day, he explained, each of us would get a slip of paper—he held one up so that we'd recognize a slip of paper when we saw one—telling us whether we'd be going to school in the morning or afternoon. We were dismissed and sent on our way.

Worse news came in general science. Near the end of the period, Miss Rheingold, red-eyed and hoarse, told us that she had resigned.

"I have been asked not to tell you why," she said, "but I hope that you will figure it out for yourselves, and when you do I hope you'll see that what I'm doing is right."

None of us knew what she was getting at, but what she said brought one big question to the collective mind of the class. Matthew asked it.

"What about our reports?"

"Well," said Miss Rheingold, "your new teacher will want to give you assignments of her own, so I guess that—"

"You mean we don't have to finish them?" asked Nicky.

"That's right," said Miss Rheingold. She seemed terribly sad.

"But I've invested considerable effort in mine," said Matthew, "and it's nearly finished."

"Well, perhaps your new teacher will let you turn it in for extra credit," said Miss Rheingold. "Or maybe she'll even want all of you to continue working on them. You can bring up the idea with her tomorrow if you like, Matthew."

"Bring it up if you'd like to experience death," muttered Nicky.

"Whatever happens," said Miss Rheingold, "I hope you'll go on thinking about your questions, and I hope you'll—"

The bell rang.

"Well," she said. "Good-bye."

I had to ask her something. I waited until everyone else had left, and then I went up to her desk.

"Miss Rheingold?" I said.

"Yes, Peter?"

"I know that all mammals sweat—perspire, I mean. And people are mammals, so people perspire."

"Very good, Peter," she said. She put her hand on my shoulder for an instant. "A syllogism. Very good."

"But when they perspire," I asked, "do they perspire from all over? I mean, do they just sweat from their foreheads and armpits, or do they perspire all over?"

"All over," she said.

"Really?" I asked. "From their heads?"

"Oh, yes," she said. "Certainly."

"And their feet?" I asked, staying wide enough of my subject not to be found out, I hoped.

"Peter," she said with a frown. "Don't you have a pair of sneakers?"

"Sure," I said.

"Then observational data ought to give you the answer to that question," she said.

"Yeah," I said. "I guess so. So people perspire from all over?"

"Yes."

"All over."

She looked at me for a moment before saying, softly, "Yes, Peter. From all over."

"Okay," I said, "and when they perspire, actual molecules of their sweat go drifting off into the air, right?"

"Right," she said.

"Thanks," I said. I held my hand out to her, she shook it, and that was our good-bye.

I wonder whether she understood what I had been getting at. I left her classroom tipsy with the idea of the conjunction of Ariane and me that occurred when we were in that little room, suspended out over the tidal stretch of the Bolotomy, watching television and breathing, something of her entering me, something of me entering her. There was a thrilling intimacy between us now, something reciprocal, something quite different from my relationship with the cabbage soup simmering on the Lodkochnikovs' kitchen stove.

Just a few minutes later, back in our homerooms, when we got our slips of paper and compared them, observational data should have shown me why Miss Rheingold had resigned. It should have, but it didn't, or, more accurately, I saw the reason, but I didn't grasp it, didn't see it for what it was. I was still only a kid, after all. I saw that Marvin wasn't going to be going to school in the same session as I would be, but I didn't see past that. When I came to school Monday afternoon, my first day back on split session, I saw the facts, but I still didn't really understand the implications. All the kids who lived in Scrub Oaks were gone. They were the ones who would be attending school in the morning, the rest of us in the afternoon. The mornings would be mostly black, the afternoons mostly white. It took me years to realize what Miss Rheingold must have seen at once. She had great legs and a penetrating mind. She had seen that split session was being used to reinstate geographical segregation. She had protested. She had been ignored. She had quit.

32

I RODE MY BIKE to the Lodkochnikovs' to tell Ariane that I wouldn't be able to watch movies with her in the afternoons anymore, but no one was home there, so I rode on down to the waterfront to see how my investment was doing. I wasn't in a particularly good mood when I walked through the door to Captain White's. I hopped onto a stool and Porky poured me a lemonade.

"I'm all ready with the sales figures," he said.

"Yeah," I said.

"It was a lot of work," he said.

"A little hard work never hurt anybody," I said, or snarled.

"Say, what's the matter with you?" said Porky.

"Never mind," I said. "I'm sorry about that crack. I know it's a lot of work. It's going to pay off, though. You'll see."

"I'm afraid I already see," said Porky. There was something grim in his voice. "I seem to see a disturbing trend."

"Oh, great," I said.

"I think that—um—as a stockholder—you'd—uh—better prepare yourself for a shock."

"A shock."

"Yeah."

"How come?"

"Because when you take a look at these figures, I think you're going to see what I see, and what I see is hamburgers."

"What?" I said.

"We sell more hamburgers than anything else," said Porky.

"Hamburgers?" I said.

"Hamburgers," he said.

"I didn't even know we were selling hamburgers."

"We just started last week."

"You didn't tell me."

"Hey, you haven't been coming in very regularly lately."

"Yeah," I said. "I've been—"

I was about to say that I'd been spending a lot of time in the Lod-kochnikovs' television room, watching movies, but that didn't sound like a good excuse for a major stockholder in Captain White's Clam Bar, so I said, "—working on my science report."

"Say, that's right!" said Porky. "How's it going?"

"It's canceled."

"Canceled?"

"Yeah." I didn't want to talk about it. "Tell me about these hamburgers."

"Well," he said, "I don't know what to say. It's got me so shook up I can't see straight. I've confronted problems before, Peter, and I've always been able to step aside from them and see right to the solution. It's uncanny, the knack I have. You throw a problem at a person and with a lot of people it's like one of those hard, hot grounders right at them, you know what I mean? They're paralyzed by it, because it's coming right at them. Well, I mean, isn't that why it *is* a problem, because it's coming right at them? But they panic. They freeze. Likely as not the ball hits them in the chin, a run scores, they're humiliated about three different ways. That doesn't happen to me. Something in me says, 'Porky, get out of the way.' So I respond to this little inner voice, and guess what? That turns out to be the secret of handling a hard, hot one—get out of the way. You take a step to one side or the other, and suddenly it's routine. It's taking that step to the side that gives you perspective on the situation. I know it. I know it, and I've done it before, but I just can't seem to do it this time."

"Start at the beginning," I said. "Maybe I can help."

"It started one afternoon last week, the very day I decided I'd better start keeping the sales records."

"You kept records only for last week?"

"I'm a busy man here, Peter," he said.

"Okay," I said. "Go ahead."

"I was standing around here waiting for somebody to walk in and order something," said Porky, "and I got to thinking about what

I was going to have for lunch myself. I looked through the menu, and I said to myself, 'I've had about as many clams as I can stand. A hamburger would sure taste good about now.' I thought I might go up to the diner and get one, but I said to myself, 'Wait a minute. Why give good money to the competition? I can buy some ground beef and cook one right here.' So that's what I did. And it was pretty good, let me tell you. I made myself some fries and onion rings to have on the side. I had forgotten to buy ketchup, so I had to use tartar sauce, which was a little odd, but still it was pretty good."

"A hamburger with tartar sauce?" I said.

"Yep," he said. "Not bad, really. Kind of exotic. I had some ground beef left, so I listed it on the menu. The Captain's Burger. Served with Tartar Sauce."

"And it's been doing well?"

"It's our best seller," he said, shaking his head. "I don't mind telling you it upsets me. I feel that this development calls my entire dream into question. My whole vision. The chain of clam stands to start with, the family-style sit-down clam restaurants after that, the sophisticated late-night clam bars, the souvenir ashtrays, the swizzle sticks with the little clams on top of them, the whole thing."

"Well, let's not worry too much yet. Let me see the figures."

"Here you go. Sorry I'm so frazzled. It's just that these hamburgers have blown me off course. I had my whole successful rise to the top of the restaurant industry mapped out. But now—"

"Are these in multiples of a hundred or something?"

"Huh?"

"A thousand?"

"What do you mean?"

"Here. Where it says 'six.' Is that six hundred or six thousand?"

"Six."

"Just six?"

"Yeah."

"Six hamburgers?"

"Yeah."

"Six?"

"Yeah."

"This is our best-selling item, and we sold six?"

"It's been a little slow."

"And what does this mean? Here—these two little lines."

"Those are sort of IOUs."

"IOUs?"

"Yeah. I owe for those."

"You bought two of these hamburgers?"

"Well, three, actually. But I figured I paid for the first one by buying the meat, you know?" His shoulders dropped as if a wet blanket had been thrown over them. "I think the dream is over, Peter," he said. "The customer is always right, you know what I mean? If they want hamburgers, and apparently they do, then hamburgers are what we ought to be giving them. I hate to have to say this to you, because I know you had faith in me when I didn't have anything but a dream, but I take a certain pride in the fact that I'm a big enough man to admit when I'm wrong, and I have to say to you now that I've been barking up the wrong tree, Peter. Clams are—well—they're a marginal snack food. They're not going to bring in the Big Money." He put his hand on my shoulder. "Peter," he said, and he swallowed hard before going on, "I think we should convert to hamburgers. One hundred percent. Turn our backs on clams. Never look back. If we really work at it, we could redecorate this place in a couple of days and then reopen with an all-hamburger decor. Maybe we could even wear little hats, like berets, in the shape of hamburgers. Say—"

"Hold it, Porky," I said. "Hold it!"

"Huh?"

"I don't think we have to worry about a hamburger trend," I said.

"No?" he said. I could see the hope in his eyes.

"No," I said. "Look at the logic of it. People can get hamburgers just about anywhere, can't they? You said yourself that you thought of going to the diner for one."

"Sure."

"So with hamburgers so readily available, do you think people would come to a place that served *nothing but* hamburgers?" I folded my arms and regarded him with a mocking smile.

"Well, they might," he said, "if—"

I was shaking my head and mouthing the word *no*.

"They wouldn't?" he said.

"No," I said. To tell the truth, I had no idea whether they would or not, but I had seen the sadness in Porky's eyes, and I knew that it came from having his plans for a lighthouse misinterpreted as a watchtower. I had seen the fear, and I knew it came from thinking that his work might collapse in a heap of scrap. "People don't want the same old thing," I said. "They're looking for something different. It may take them some time to realize it, but they will."

"Really?"

"Sure," I said. "If we went a hundred percent hamburger, we'd lose our shirts."

"You really think so?" he asked.

"I do," I said. "Besides, you're misinterpreting the data."

"I am?"

"Yes. Look. You personally accounted for half of the hamburger sales. And you didn't take into account the fact that everything else on the menu has clams in it. So you and three other people bought hamburgers. Everybody else came in here for clams."

"You're right," he said, wiping the back of his hand across his brow. "Why didn't I see that? What's wrong with me?"

"Nothing's wrong with you," I said.

"No?" he said. "Something like that right under my nose and I don't even *see* it? And you think nothing's wrong with me?"

"I think it was probably just a temporary blindness," I said. "Your vision was kind of blinded by—um—a craving. You had hamburgers on your mind, and that blinded you to the obvious. You know how that can happen. Sometimes you get hungry for one specific thing, and nothing else will satisfy that hunger, like—"

"Women."

"I was going to say toasted marshmallows," I said, "but I guess it's the same principle. You just get so that you can't think of anything but toasted marshmallows."

"Or women," he said. "I see what you're getting at. It gets so bad sometimes I seem to see beautiful women *everywhere*. You know what I mean?"

"Sure," I said. I was *beginning* to know what he meant. "Anyway," I said, "I think we should forget about hamburgers. There are just too many places selling hamburgers already."

"You might be right," he said. "I *know* you're right about that craving business. You get hungry for them, and it's as if the wom-

en you see every day had suddenly undergone some kind of transformation. A metamorphosis. Wham! All of a sudden they *all*
look gorgeous. But, as you said, it's just a kind of blindness
brought on by hunger."

"Maybe," I said. "Anyway, I know I'm right about this. Since
just about every diner sells hamburgers, people are not going to go
out of their way to drive to *another* place that sells hamburgers. I
tell you, Porky, we'd lose our shirts."

"Of course we would," he said. "I don't know what came over
me. It must have been what you said, a hunger, just a craving.
Blurred my vision, distorted it, just like seeing beautiful women
everywhere. But wait!" he said, brightening suddenly. "That re-
minds me—that craving might have paid off. Not the hamburger
one, the other one." He poked me with his finger and winked. "Before I went into hamburger blindness," he said, "I had an idea. An
excellent idea. Excellent. It's going to make us the big money.
Take a look at this."

From under the counter he produced what at first I took for a pillow. It was covered with fuzzy gray material, and its shape closely
resembled the fuzzy photographs of flying saucers that appeared in
newspapers every week or so at that time. When I spotted the eyes,
I realized that it was a stuffed-animal version of a clam.

"I made it myself," said Porky.

"It's a pillow?" I asked.

"It's a hat," he said, disappointed. He showed me the elastic
strap. "For the waitress."

"We're going to have a waitress?"

"We *have* a waitress. She starts this afternoon. In fact," he said,
raising his eyes toward the door, his expression brightening considerably, "here she comes now." He called out, "Hey, you're late."

"I had to get the skirt," said a familiar voice. I turned toward the
door. Ariane was entering.

"Ariane?" I said.

"Hi, Peter," she said.

"You're going to be a waitress here? *The* waitress here?"

"Starting today," she said.

"But what about Babbington Clam?"

"I didn't like the hours," she said. "Starting at seven in the morning? Forget it! Here I'll work three to ten—my parents'll be asleep by the time I get home. And it's like a party every day here!"

"It is?" I said, looking toward Porky.

"Sure," he said quickly. "Not when you're here, Peter, but later. Dinner time—and later than that—at night. We get a great bunch of kids in here then. Ariane's going to have a blast."

I looked at the sales figures again. They didn't suggest that there was ever much of a "bunch" at Captain White's at all.

"Go put the skirt on, Ariane," said Porky. "Use the ladies' room."

"Okay," she said.

"She's going to draw the boys the way honey draws flies," said Porky. "When word gets around, this place will be packed at night. It *will* be like a party."

"Yeah, I guess you're right," I said. "She'll probably have a good time, too. It's just that—"

I couldn't have told Porky what was bothering me; it was the discovery that Ariane was willing to give up our movie afternoons to work here. I had just lost those afternoons to split session anyway, but *she* didn't know that. She'd been willing to give them up for a job as a waitress in a clam joint. Ariane came out of the ladies' room wearing a tight sweater and a little skater's skirt.

"How do you like it?" she asked.

"Very nice," said Porky. "Here, put this on." He gave her the hat he'd made. She put it on her head, fiddled with the chin strap, and finally ended up with the clam perched on the right side of her head, tilted forward a little, so that his goofy eyes seemed to stare down at you when you looked into her face. Porky made a twirling gesture with his finger, Ariane spun around, and the skirt flared out and showed us her legs.

"What do you think, Peter?" asked Porky.

"Very nice," I said, but I took a bitter consolation from the realization that, though Ariane's legs were cute enough, if legs were electrons, Miss Rheingold's would orbit on a higher level altogether.

33

I SPENT SOME TIME feeling sorry for myself. I had no Miss
Rheingold, no Ariane, no intriguing science project to give my life
direction and meaning. I told myself that I shouldn't regret the loss
of Ariane because she certainly was increasing the value of my
stock in Porky's venture even if she wasn't enriching my afternoons, but I couldn't find any compensation at all for the loss of
Miss Rheingold and the science project. What good was the Big
Money without the Big Questions? The project had filled my time
for so long that without it I hardly knew what to do with myself.
Rambling through the encyclopedia seemed entirely purposeless
with no science report to write, so I wandered there less and less. I
had nothing better to do now, so I gave in to Raskol and Marvin's
urging and began working with them to rebuild the watchtower.

In our absence, of course, the bamboo had overgrown the site
we'd cleared, so we had to begin by hacking it back. The three of
us had been hacking at it for a while when Guppa suddenly burst
into the little clearing we'd made.

"We're on!" he said.

"On?" I said.

"We're going to be on 'Fantastic Contraptions.'" He handed a
letter to me. It was true. He and Mrs. Jones had been chosen "from
literally thousands of applicants" the letter said.

"This is great!" I said.

"We urge you," the letter went on, "not to confuse appearing on
the show with winning. There can be only one winner each program, and the audience alone determines which inventor that is."

I read that part, but I didn't pay any attention to it. Of *course,* I confused being on the show with winning.

"LET'S MAKE A PARTY of it," I said. "We can all get together to watch the show when they're on—us, and Gumma, and the Joneses, and—"

"No, I don't think so, Peter," said my father.

"Aw, come on," I said. "It can be a real victory celebration, with everybody together, and we could have some of Mrs. Jones's gumbo and you could make some tuna casserole, Mom, and Gumma could make chicken fricassee—"

I was hopping around, full of Guppa and Mrs. Jones's certain victory, anticipating the pleasure of the victory feast, suggesting dishes, but my parents were ignoring me. Finally, when I wouldn't shut up about the fun we were all going to have, my father said, "Peter, that's enough. We are not going to have any victory celebration."

"Aw gee—"

"'Aw, gee,' nothing. For one thing, we don't know that Herb and What's-her-name—"

"Mrs. Jones."

"Mrs. Jones. We don't know that they're going to win. And it isn't wise to count your chickens before they're hatched."

"And for another thing?"

"What?"

"And for another thing. You said 'for one thing.' What's the other thing?"

"Never mind. Finish your lima beans."

Later, when I was upstairs in my room, lying in the dark, sulking, I heard my parents talking in the living room. Little by little my father's voice grew louder, until I could make out what he was saying; it was, "I have nothing against them, I just don't want one in my house."

I knew what he meant. I got out of bed. I wasn't aware that I had a plan, but I think I felt that I had to see him, to judge the expression on his face, before I could be sure that what I thought of him was justified. I went partway down the stairs and sat down at the point where the wall ended. From this spot I could peek through the balusters and see my parents, sitting at the far end of the living room. There was my father, slumped in his overstuffed chair, a small man, diminished by his attitudes, hurt, frightened, angry. I shifted slightly, and the stair creaked. He looked up. I don't know whether he could see me or not through the balusters, but for a moment it seemed that our eyes locked. I felt a thrill similar to that I had felt in the locker, hiding from the watchman, the thrill of danger, the danger of being found out, for here it seemed to me that if my father saw me, he would also see into me, he would know what I thought of him, what I was thinking of him. He could still save things between us. It wasn't too late. He could change his mind now. He could declare that he was wrong. He kept his eyes on me for what seemed like a long while, and I froze there, in an awkward position, with the toes of one foot bent back, all my weight on that foot, not breathing.

Then he turned his eyes back toward the television set, his face sour and grim, and he said nothing. I waited, and I waited some more, hoping that he would speak, but he didn't, and after a while I began to get a cramp from holding the same position for so long, and then I began to see that he never would say that he was wrong, because he thought he was right. In fact, he wasn't thinking at all, merely feeling. Everything between us was ruined. From then on I would think less and less of him, grow more and more convinced that he was a fool. Our future was doomed.

Slowly I began to rise from my cramped position. I was going to creep back to bed, leave my father sitting there in silence, tiny in his comfortable chair, his range circumscribed by the limits of his own mind, his thinking hobbled by his fears, his views nothing but a hodgepodge of suppositions and superstitions, but then, before I'd even stood fully, something happened.

Who can say exactly what it was? Perhaps a cosmic ray, zipping along through space, passed at that moment through the atmosphere, through the roof of our house, through my bedroom upstairs, through the floor and ceiling, through my father's skull, and into his brain, where it knocked out of its orbit a single electron in a single atom of his hippocampus, the seat of memory, conviction, and superstition, causing a tiny imbalance of electrical potential between two neurons, just enough to make those neurons fire across their synapse, exciting other neurons, which fired, exciting others, which fired, and so on, until neurons were firing all over the place, like mousetraps on a Ping-Pong table, and all my father's wrongheaded ideas were flushed from his hippocampus and dissipated into nowhere, into the *Zwischenraum*, transforming him in an eyeblink from an unthinking bigot to a true *homo sapiens*, something like the sudden conversion Mr. Lodkochnikov experienced when he finally decided to buy a television set—or maybe the stair creaked as I stood up. Whatever it was, something happened to him. He seemed to snap. He sat up. He shuddered. He wore a look of surprise. He peered the length of the room, narrowed his eyes, frowned. He swallowed, and frowned again. Maybe it was heartburn. He turned to the television set again, but in a moment he looked toward my mother, and then he got up out of his chair and turned the set off. He spoke, apparently to my mother, as if there had been no pause, as if he'd been speaking to her all along.

"At least that's the way I used to feel," he said. "But, you know, Ella, maybe I've been wrong."

"Huh," said my mother, who must have wondered what he was talking about. I knew.

"I was looking at myself in the mirror down at the end of the room, and I don't like what I see."

My mother looked that way.

"I look small, so small, a poor man sitting in a big chair in the light of that stupid television set. He seems too small, this poor man. Small. And frightened. A prisoner of his own fears."

My mother was starting to look a little frightened herself.

"He's one of those people who's ruled by emotion rather than thought, you know what I mean?"

My mother shook her head. Her mouth was open.

"He lets himself believe things that he doesn't really know. That's me, maybe. Maybe. Maybe I've let myself become a slave to irrational beliefs."

"Bert," said my mother.

"No, Ella," said my father. "Let me go on. I think I let myself

get sucked into a kind of ignorant tribalism. It's like—it's like—
it's like cumulative error. Do you know what that is?"

"No," said my mother.

I had heard all I needed to hear. I crept back upstairs and got into
bed. Below, I could hear my father explaining cumulative error to my
mother. I fell asleep, content, secure in the knowledge that whatever
had changed my father had changed our future. I wasn't going to have
to hold that earlier moment against him for the rest of our lives. I
wasn't going to have to hate him.

34

I THINK IT WAS THE BIGGEST gathering we had ever had in my house. It seemed as if everyone I knew was there—except Guppa and Mrs. Jones, of course. They had driven in to the city early in the morning, so that they'd be in the studio, with their demonstration waterwillow set up, well before "Fantastic Contraptions" went on the air. These were still the days of live television. We'd be watching the show as it happened.

Everyone had taken the day off. It felt like a national holiday. Throughout the morning, people had come by with television sets. There were several in the living room, a couple in the kitchen, and four on the dining room table. No matter where you were, you wouldn't miss the show. There was a lot of chatter and eating, but I was too nervous to do anything but sit in front of one of the sets and wait for the show to come on. At last it did. The theme, a novelty number with pennywhistles and kazoos and gongs, hushed everyone, and from then on anyone who spoke, even to praise Guppa and Mrs. Jones, was the target of shushing from all sides.

They were the last contestants, preceded by a woman who had invented a bathtub that automatically washed a dog, a child prodigy with a multiple pantograph that allowed him to write "I will not scratch my fingernail on the blackboard" a hundred times with one motion of its master pencil, and a man with a model of a microscope that he claimed could show details smaller than any observed before. The people gathered in my house were worried by this last contestant, because his gadget seemed to have real merit, but I knew that he didn't have a chance. While he was explaining how the microscope worked, why it had higher resolving power than conventional microscopes, and describing the limits imposed by the wavelength of the light, Freddie actually yawned. The microscope just wasn't funny. He was sure to come in last. I was more worried about the lady with the dog-washer. The dog had squirmed and howled while it was being washed and finally leaped from the tub and shook water all over Flo. The crowd loved it. That could be trouble.

At last, it was Guppa and Mrs. Jones's turn.

"Now, Flo and Freddie," said the announcer, "here are our final contestants for today, from Babbington, Long Island, here are Marie Jones and Herb Piper!"

"Well, hello there," said Freddie. "Marie Jones. Herb Piper. Marie, may I call you Marie?"

"Oh, yes," said Mrs. Jones. "Please do."

"But call me Herb," said Guppa.

This brought on a kind of sucking noise in my house. I think people were embarrassed that Guppa had said something a little foolish. The audience in the studio loved it, though. We were off to a great start.

"All right," said Freddie, laughing along with his audience. "If you insist."

"Marie and Herb," said Flo. "Tell us a little about yourselves—are you—married?"

"Oh, yes," said Mrs. Jones

"But, uh, not to each other," said Guppa.

"Really!" said Flo. More laughter. "I see!" She paused to let the laughter subside, then leaned toward Guppa and Mrs. Jones and asked, "Do your spouses know that you've slipped out together like this?"

"Huh?" said Guppa. "Oh, sure. In fact, my wife, Lorna, helped us quite a bit."

"And my husband," said Mrs. Jones. "Howard."

"Well, that's good," said Freddie. "We wouldn't want to get you into any trouble." People were roaring now. We were a cinch.

"Marie and Herb," said Freddie, "why don't you explain for the people just what your invention does."

"Well," said Guppa, "it waters your garden automatically."

"Yes," said Flo, "I see you have a water sprinkler there."

"That's right, Flo," said Guppa. "That's a standard water sprinkler."

"And attached to it—" said Flo.

"You can get a water sprinkler like that just about anywhere," said Guppa.

"Right," said Flo. "Attached to it I see you have—"

"I got this one at a hardware store right in Babbington," said Guppa.

"I'll bet that's where you got the hose, too," said Freddie.

"That's right," said Guppa, nodding his head. "Right at Babbington Supply."

"Trash-can lid, too, I bet," said Freddie.

Still nodding, Guppa said, "They've got just about everything you need."

By now, the audience was laughing nearly continuously, and I figured that we were nearly there, but then came the crowning touch, more than I could have hoped for. Flo extended a long-nailed finger toward one of Mrs. Jones's windflowers. The camera showed a close-up. Flo flicked the windflower, and it spun and shone in the studio lights. We saw a close-up of Flo's face. She was suppressing a laugh. "What do you call this?" she asked.

"A windflower," said Mrs. Jones.

"And what do you call the whole thing?" asked Freddie.

"A waterwillow," said Mrs. Jones.

"So this is a waterwillow with windflowers?" said Freddie. "Waterwillow with windflowers, waterwillow with windflowers, waterwillow with windflowers. Whew! My wips are weawy!" There was no way we could lose now.

"What are these windflowers for, Marie?" asked Flo.

"Oh, they look pretty," said Mrs. Jones. "And chickens like that sort of thing."

"*Chickens*?" shouted Flo. The audience roared.

"Yes," said Mrs. Jones. "Chickens enjoy watching anything that spins and catches the light."

"Not only does it water your garden!" said Freddie, "It entertains your chickens! Wow! Say, Flo, didn't your uncle have some chickens—" and they were off. The rest was anticlimax. I knew that Guppa and Mrs. Jones would win. They'd made Flo and Freddie laugh, and that was what it took.

They won a set of camping equipment, everything from tent to mess kit, including a hefty cylindrical battery-operated camp lantern with a lens that could focus its beam from floodlight to spotlight. When Raskol noticed it in the array of prizes, he nudged Marvin and me and said, "Hey! That's the perfect thing for the watchtower."

35

RASKOL AND MARVIN AND I put to use the lessons we had learned from our earlier failure. When we were finished building Watchtower II, we had a solid base from which a dozen long uprights rose, tapering inward to support a smaller platform at the top. We made a ladder by nailing crosspieces to two of the uprights, and when, after climbing the ladder to the top, we found that the structure exhibited familiar tendencies toward collapse, we broke down and sought Guppa's advice. He taught us the technique of triangular bracing.

While we were building and bracing the tower, we developed the game. I had never imagined that any game would be played in the lighthouse that I had originally designed. I just expected to sit up there and keep the light turning, letting my mind wander, and alerting any ships that might otherwise have blundered the five miles inland to my neighborhood, but it wasn't a lighthouse any longer. Now it was a watchtower, and a watchtower was something else. As Raskol pointed out, it seemed to demand a watchman and some kind of action, along the lines of a prison break, with a guard in the watchtower who picked off prisoners as they tried to make a dash from the base of the tower into the concealing darkness of my back yard. We tried some thought experiments, playing this escape game in our minds, and it just didn't work. If the prisoners tried to escape one at a time, the guard was sure to get them all, and if they made a mass break, too many succeeded. There were either too many losers or too many winners. I don't know who suggested that the situation be reversed, but as soon as we thought of it we saw that it was the logical way to play. People would try to break *into* the tower.

In the game that we came to call Night Watchman, there was a single watchman, who climbed the crude ladder to the upper platform, where he sat beside the rotating light, the camp light that had been part of the loot Guppa and Mrs. Jones had won, mounted on the windup record player. The watchman was armed with a long, multicell flashlight, the beam of which was supposed to be deadly. There could be any number of other players. They became what we called called night crawlers, or just crawlers. The watchman's object was to keep the crawlers out of the tower. We didn't supply any reason for the crawlers' wanting to get into the tower or for the watchman's wanting to keep them out. Their having conflicting goals was just part of the nature of the game, part of the nature of things: crawlers want to get into the tower; the watchman wants to keep them out. That's the way it is. To start the game, the watchman closed his eyes and counted to a hundred while the crawlers scattered into the back yard. Then the watchman wound the record player and released the brake. The revolving searchlight swept the yard, and the watchman watched for the approaching crawlers while, inch by inch, they made their way through the weeds, over open patches of lawn, around shrubs, and through paths cut in the bamboo toward the base of the tower. A crawler who made it into the tower was a winner, and a crawler who was caught in the searchlight beam or the beam of the watchman's flashlight was a loser. The game wasn't over for the losers, though. They—and, for reasons I don't recall, the winners as well—joined the watchman on the upper platform and helped him spot crawlers. We played each night's game until it was over, until all the crawlers had gotten into the tower or been caught in the attempt. In practice, the end often came sooner, when our parents demanded that we come in for the night, but in theory there was no time limit. The game wasn't over until the last crawler had been caught or made it into the tower.

The first night we played Night Watchman, Marvin was the watchman. There must have been thirty crawlers in my back yard, trying to get into the tower without being caught. Most of them weren't very good at avoiding detection. They snapped twigs, sneezed, stood up if the tricky watchman called their names, asked for time out to go to the bathroom, and were caught in the beam of the watchman's flashlight every time. Impatience was their common fault. They got twitchy. Those of us who learned to play the game well discovered that it was a waiting game. A crawler had to be willing to lie perfectly still for long periods of time, waiting for the watchman to shift position, for a car to honk its horn somewhere, for another crawler to make an error, for anything that would cover the sound of an inch's progress toward the tower, and had to enjoy the idea that the game had no time limit.

After a couple of weeks, Raskol, Marvin, and I were the only ones who still played the game regularly. There were always other kids playing with us, but they came and went and never amounted to more than static. We three, however, had become passionate devotees. I was a masterly crawler, and proud of it. I had had some training. My idle days in the field where the Purlieu Street School now stood had taught me crawling. My afternoons beside Ariane had taught me the art of inching up. Most of all though, I had a new knack for patience. I was so good at being patient that I amazed myself. I learned the trick from my encyclopedia ramblings; my secret consisted mainly of letting my mind wander while I waited for an opening, rambling from thought to thought as a way of keeping myself from growing impatient and making a mistake that would reveal me. If I waited, my time would come. So I would lie in wait and think, deliberately think. A word might get me going, or a memory, but every time I'd find myself wandering from one thought to another.

I think my preference for working in small bites began with this game, this lying in the dark and thinking about something for a while and then moving on to something suggested by it. When I think hard about something, pay really close attention to it, I can sustain the effort only for short bits. At the level of really close attention, my mind is working too fast, like the windup record player when I had it operating at its highest possible speed, and there seems to be some danger of a rattling collapse—best to slow it down for a while. However, operating always at a comfortable speed, looking always at the surface of things, thinking at the level of generalities,

wouldn't be satisfactory. Nothing really interesting can be compre-
hended at that level without simplifying it to the point where it's no
longer particularly interesting at all, and what would be the good of
examining something interesting, anything interesting—for example, making observations of your personal history, adventures, and
experiences—at such a gross level of perception? At the grosser
levels of perception, you see surfaces, you see edges, and you seem
to see mostly differences, boundaries where things are differentiated
from one another, but for short, tiring periods you can get down to
the finer levels, working with extremely fine tools, set at fantastic
degrees of magnification. When you look at yourself—or anything—that closely, you are looking at tiny bits, each of which
yields only a tinier bit of information. You absorb it, consider it,
and move on to the next tiny bit. You may have to take some time
at the surface to catch your breath, change your leaky batteries, re-
wind your spring, but you'll be back. You are an explorer of the
minuscule, and the picture you begin to form is busy and bumpy,
not at all the smooth and regular impression you got from a greater
distance, or at a lower magnification. Down here differences are
harder to see. As Quanto the Minimum and *Elementary Introductory Physics Made Easy for Beginners (Book One)* taught me, things
get strange down among the tiny bits. Sometimes things overlap,
and it's hard to tell whose electron is whose, hard to tell where one
edge stops and another starts, hard to tell when you've stopped
thinking about one idea and started on another.

Thoughts like that—not that one specifically, of course, but
thoughts like it—kept me quiet in the dark until the time was right
to wriggle closer to the tower.

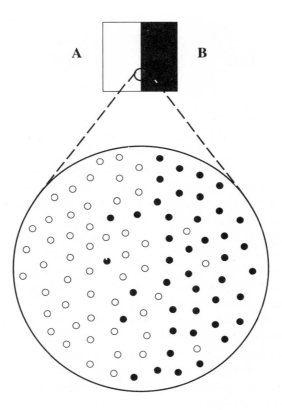

Figure 7: A gross, macroscopic view (top) apparently shows a sharp line of demarcation between two regions, A and B. However, a closer look (bottom) shows that things are not so simple. The regions may represent the sweat and oils on the skin of a seventeen-year-old-woman (A) and an eleven-year-old boy (B) commingling when they touch; an advancing cloud of perfume (A) penetrating the ambient atmosphere of a general science classroom (B); the end of one episode in a person's life (A) and the beginning of another (B); some members of the white population of a place like Babbington (A) mingling with the black population (B); a grove of bamboo (A) advancing on a field of wheat (B); children in elementary school drifting from one subject (A) to the next (B) in the years before they are made to change classes; and the way, when we let our minds wander, one idea (A) dissolves into the next (B), like the edges of objects depicted in a watercolor painting.

36

ONE NIGHT, I was lying in the young bamboo at the foot of the hill, waiting, watching for an opportunity, letting my thoughts ramble to keep myself from growing impatient and giving myself away.

Raskol was on the tower, and Marvin, who had been caught, was beside him. The turntable was running down, the beam from the lantern circling slower and slower. Raskol rewound the motor, and under cover of the noise of the rewinding I crawled forward a bit. The light began to sweep around again.

With the patience of a champion crawler, I settled in for as long as it might take until the time was right for another move. The water in the trash-can lid hanging from one of the waterwillows evaporated enough to turn Guppa's automatic watering device on, the little bits of tin began whirring and clattering when droplets hit them, and I was able to cover a couple of feet before it shut off again. Thanks, waterwillow. *Waterwillow*, one of my favorite words. I let my mind drift, and I was soon off on a ramble, like Flo and Freddie taking off from one of the superfluous doodads on a fantastic contraption, or my own cross-referential rambles through the encyclopedia. *Waterwillows*. All of us watching Guppa and Mrs. Jones on "Fantastic Contraptions," staring at the silver light, the light that lit up Ariane's hip. Her perfume. *Diffusion*, another of my favorites. The intriguing aroma of Ariane, diffusing in the little room, the diffusing scent of Miss Rheingold's perfume. *Depreciation*, the diffusion of a Studebaker. *Bun soup, windflowers, court bouillon, Zwischenraum, shandy, ontology, epistemology, bills of lading—*

I was going to laugh. I had come to a thought that was going to make me laugh. I bit my lip, but that made the thought all the clearer, the pressure of the laugh all the greater. A little of it escaped from me, as a snort, a small, ambiguous sound. Raskol's flashlight swung in my direction, but it missed me, and in missing me reminded me all the more of the watchman's light, of hiding in the locker, and—

I couldn't hold it. I burst out laughing, and Raskol shone the beam full in my face.

"Got you," he said. "What's so funny?"

"*Splines!*" I cried.

37

BECAUSE THE UNIVERSE IS EXPANDING, and, as Quanto pointed out, most of everything is nothing, every day, every moment, more nothing separates the rest. With more and more *Zwischenraum*, the universe is becoming more and more transparent. When Raskol sprayed me with that beam of photons from the flashlight, some of them were reflected outward, arranged in a pattern imposed on them by the contours of my face. Many of them never made it out of the atmosphere, of course—they collided with molecules of this and that, got transmuted, caused transmutations—but the number of photons in that beam was enormous, and lots of them got away. Observational evidence tells us that must be the case. Just as the observational evidence of the odor of sneakers tells us that we sweat from our feet, the fact that spy satellites can read the numbers on license plates shows us that lots of photons make their way through the atmosphere. From there on, the odds that the photons reflected from me would survive got better and better, and the odds in their favor have improved every day, and continue to improve, as their obstacles drift farther and farther apart in the expanding universe, making it a little more likely every day, every moment, that at least some of them will continue rushing on and on, for something like forever, or as close to forever as the universe itself will ever come. Those commemorative photons were all traveling at the same speed when they left my face, and the survivors have all continued traveling at the same speed, of course, since there is no adjusting screw on light. Therefore, some trace of their pattern, the image of my face, has been preserved and will be preserved as long as any of them are still racing outward undisturbed, undeflected, and so, perhaps, in that one sense, there is no end of me, I do not stop. That stream of endlessly rushing photons commemorates me and that moment, since they carry in their pattern an image of me then. Though that cosmic snapshot is vastly diffused now, it may very well have endured, and if it has, then in that gang of photons must reside, though no one is capable of seeing it, an eternal image of me, caught in the moment when I lay there on my back in the bamboo, laughing, and that image of me rushes outward still, thirty-five light-years away now, the image of my eleven-year-old self, laughing in spite of myself when my rambling mind made its way backward word by delicious word to *splines,* the word that made me laugh out loud, since it brought with it a memory bound to it as it has been ever since, the memory of the day school ended for the summer, when Raskol and Marvin and I slipped into our lockers at the end of the day, remained in hiding there for hours—until the watchman passed on his rounds and settled down to eat his dinner and the halls were as empty and echoing as they had been before the school opened—and then emerged from our lockers and, silently, biting our lips to stifle our laughter, to save it, to plant it for harvesting in September, changed the combinations of the locks.

Respectfully submitted, Miss Rheingold, wherever you are.

(TO BE CONTINUED)